I0743244

# KURT DANGER:

## RETIRED MONSTER HUNTER

## LEROI R. REED

Henceforth Publishing Co.

# Table of Contents

# Chapter One
# LAST CALL

In an old bar, the kind of bar with old bar stools in desperate need of reupholstery, where the smell of years of dried up beer stained the air. The bartender tries to wake up his last customer.

"Wake up Kurt!" He shoves a drunk and tired old man who is hopefully still alive. The man is having dreams of winged creatures part flesh part stone flying towards him and he grabs his gun preparing to blast them away. The bartender shoves him again, this time the man wakes up looking at the spilled mug then at the bartender, "Sorry Ted."

"No problem Kurt just closing up now, you need a ride?"

Kurt wipes his face, drops cash, and gets up.

"No, I'm going to walk."

"In this rain?"

"Yep. See you soon Ted." He exits the Bar and begins to walk.

Walking in the pouring rain, in a tattered black leather jacket, his hair is wild and accompanied by a scruffy salt and pepper beard. There was a look of solemn embedded in his eyes. Standing at about 6'1 and 235-ish pounds, the years have him beat from constant fighting. He walks past drug addicts, the homeless, and the occasional drunken, privileged idiot just leaving the expensive clubs. He hears a woman scream, then a loud smack coming from the dark alley across the street. He looks in that direction, thinks about intervening, then shakes his head and continues on his way. Then he hears the laughter of three men, and the whimper of a young woman. Not my problem, he reminds himself.

Then he hears one of the men say, "I'm going to have a little fun with you, right before I rip your pretty little throat out". That triggers something in Kurt, his eyes fill with rage, as he stops, he knows just what's about to happen and he cannot ignore it anymore. Walking across the street to the alley trying to be quiet, he sees three men punching and kicking a woman. One of the men is a skinny pencil faced man with a strong body odor and this punk rocker look about him. They begin to grow from the tips of his teeth as one of them is prepping to strike her neck when he hears,

"Hey, fang face."

He turns around to see the old man standing in the alleyway entrance. He begins to laugh at him, "Get lost old man before we kill you."

Kurt laughs, "Old? Listen Fang Face. I'm going to give you and your other bloodsucking friends over there to the count of five to leave the girl alone and leave without getting hurt."

The vampires begin to laugh, the one seeming to be the leader is still laughing when he says, "Are you fucking kidding me? You hear that guys? He wants us to leave before we get hurt." Kurt stays firm. "5."

Their laughter fills the alley, "4".

The leader bares his fangs at Kurt and points at the other two, "Hold her and don't let her out of your sight while I deal with the old fart."

"3."

The leader stops turning back towards Kurt, "Are you fucking serious?"

Kurt smiles and says, "2."

The leader runs at Kurt with blinding speed leaping into the air ready to pounce him, Kurt whips out his beloved pistols Death and Taxes and fires two Hellfire bullets into his skull. He disintegrates into a pile of ash and scatters in the air.

Kurt whispers as the smoking ash clears, "1."

Shock forms across their faces as the legend himself, Kurt Danger, dawns on them. As the others try to run away, he shoots both of them, reducing them to the same fate as their leader. The young lady lays there shaking as reality sets in.

"You can get up now."

Adrenaline running through her, and ignoring him, she gets up and runs to the first pile of ash and grabs the pants, digging in them for her stuff. "Fuck yeah."

As she pulls out a small bag of cocaine, Kurt turns away disgusted as he realizes he just saved a drug addict from a drug deal gone bad. As he walks away his words drift back to her. "Should've let 'em kill you."

She screams back at him, "Fuck you, old man!"

*****

After a long walk, Kurt finally ends up at the apartment he hates. It's a seemingly underwhelming place with no real furniture except an old recliner. There are no pictures or any-thing hanging up on the wall. No television. No coffee table. Nothing–not a thing–to resemble a home.

Grabbing a few beers out of his equally bare fridge, he sits down on his chair, cracks it open, and begins to drink. Four or five beers in and Kurt is knocked out (dreaming about his old job and thinking about the vampires).

You may be wondering who this guy is and why should you care. Well, his name is Kurt Danger, and five years ago he was the greatest monster hunter to ever do the job. These days though, he goes by Kurt Dawson–a name he despises almost as much as his apartment. I know you're probably thinking,

what in the world happened to this great monster destroyer. I mean they don't still exist right? As a matter of fact, they're very real, some are walking amongst us every day and people like you are none the wiser. Are you still someone who subscribes to the notion that the government isn't hiding any secrets, and whatever they do is for our own "safety"?

If you answered yes to any of those, then stop reading this right now, and you can go on being happy with your naïve life. They say ignorance is bliss and I won't be the one to burst your bubble. But if you answered no, well then, I got some news you'd like to hear.

Centuries ago, whenever there was a murder that was deemed a "run in" with a vicious animal, or someone was killed by an "undetermined cause," the government officials of that time would send in specialized groups called monster hunters. These Elite groups would consist of scientists and bounty hunters whose purpose was to seek out the threat, eliminate the threat, and cover it all up to protect the world from knowledge of real monsters.

Unfortunately, that's where our story begins; Kurt's family was a victim of a vicious vampire slaughter when he was but a wee lad. He was orphaned and taken in by a monster hunter known simply as Mr. Danger. Along with his hatred for the beasts that killed his parents, Kurt was taught how to kill every single monster known to man—from werewolves and gargoyles to vampires and ghouls. Successfully, at the age of 13, he was skilled in hand-to-hand combat, as well as archery, and the use of various firearms, rifles, and explosives. At 13, he had already killed his first vampire, and at 15 he had broken the record of killing the most vampires in one room. He was a legend by his early 20s, and an unstoppable force when it came to monster hunting. When Mr. Danger retired, Kurt took on his mentor and friend's mantle and became known as Kurt Danger. For years that name would strike fear in anything evil's heart, until one night, Danger would be struck with a career ending tragedy.

*****

Kurt was in a grand ballroom, standing in the middle of this ballroom with a ripped white shirt and black leather jacket. He had his favorite weapons out still smoking from his last shots where there are piles of ash and fancy clothes littered around him. He looks up and screams,

"Vexor! Get your ass out here and face me, you weak, blood-sucking leech!"

Tremendous clapping greets him; the balcony doors swing open to reveal more guests of this well-dressed affair and their host Vexor, the crowned Prince of the Family of V. He comes out laughing and applauding with his guests.

"Kurt... quite the show. Man, you simply are the baddest motherfucker of all time. I mean you really live up to all those stories about you." Turning towards his guests.

"Believe the hype people, this is the real deal. Unfortunately, this actually wasn't part of the evening's planned extracurricular activities." Vexor's entertained smirk contorts into a face of disgust. He glares at Kurt, "You crashed my fucking party, slaughtered my guests, and ruined my dance floor." Vexor holds

his hand gesturing to the piles of ash around Kurt. "...And for what, huh? 'Cause I killed your little fiancée?"

Kurt screams in rage and begins shooting in his direction, firing his last bullets. Instead of it hitting his target, several other vampires move in to take the bullets for Vexor. Kurt finally hears himself shooting empty clips and drops to the floor in defeat. He has failed to get the revenge he sought, and he knows it. Vexor laughs and speaks to him tauntingly. "Don't worry Kurt, I am going to hurt you real bad. But first these guys are going to really fuck you up."

Five vampires dressed in black military gear step from behind several curtains on the balcony area surrounding Kurt. He hears Vexor continues. "...but after they do all that, I'm going to plunge that bitch's sword right through your heart so you can be together again." He laughs hysterically and the vampires converge on Kurt.

Suddenly a phone rings, and Kurt wakes up from his nightmare. The phone goes to voicemail.

"Kurt, we need to talk A.S.A.P. so meet me at our usual table. Baxter should be on his way right now." Kurt looks at the clock, the phone rings again, he gets up and walks inside of a closet. As he puts on a clean white tee shirt, Kurt picks up, "Hey old man, did you get a call from Sam?"

"Hey Baxter. Yeah, just got the voicemail. I'm heading there now. How far out are you?"

"Not too far out… making a stop first along route 60, so I'll meet you around there. Hey just so you know, word is the Mashers have you on their radar again. You gotta be careful Kurt."

"Yeah, yeah, alright. I'll pick you up around Route 60 in about an hour. I gotta pick up Black Beauty." The phone went silent.

Kurt opens his closet to reveal more guns and ammo boxes. He grabs his black duffle bag and begins to pack up. He grabs his keys, the last two beers, and walks out the door right into his landlord, "Leaving quite early, aren't you Mr. Dawson? Do you have my rent?" Kurt shakes his head and imagining himself knocking her head clean off with a spiked bat. He smiles and says, "No, but you'll have it tonight." He walks away knowing that he wouldn't be back tonight or ever. As he walks to his car, he regretted not telling her to fuck off.

*****

Kurt walks into Manny's Auto Shop, a dirty little hole in the wall auto mechanic shop. Manny does the dirty jobs no one else can and he has stored away his "baby" before with Manny. Kurt walks around shouting Manny's name trying to find the old mechanic. Finally, Manny comes from under a car covered in oil and dirt.

"Was wondering when you'd be back for that Black Beauty of yours."

"Hey Manny, look I can't talk long. Here's the rest I owe you with a little extra." Kurt says, tossing an envelope to Manny. Getting up, Manny catches it.

"She's back here, I fixed the interior like you asked. The bullet holes were easy enough to fix and it runs smooth like a baby now. I even reinforced the body so, unless you're taking on a tank, you should be okay."

They turn a corner and under a silver sheet in the garage area lies Kurt's Black Beauty. Manny removes the cover and Kurt smiles, "Nice job Manny... she looks brand new... like her first day home."

Manny puts his hands on his hips and smiles back. Kurt gets in, Manny comes to the side window and asks, "You headed on some secret mission?"

Kurt grabs his black shades out of the glove box and puts them on, turns to Manny and says, "Nope. Headed to see an old friend, that's all. Be safe Manny. Anyone comes here looking for me, you don't know me, and you haven't seen me." Kurt pulls off and drives into the night.

A few miles down the road, Kurt decides to stop to fuel up on gas and grab more beers. He walks into the small and vacant Quick Mart and grabs two six packs. He shuffles over to the counter and points to a pack of Newport 100's behind the cashier. While the cashier grabs his cigarettes, three very hairy, smelly, and dingy-looking individuals walk through the door. Kurt immediately recognizes their familiar scent, the smell of wet dog and dry blood—werewolves. He tries not to draw their attention. This place isn't big enough for a battle with 3 full-grown werewolves. Even if they're not strong or fast they'd still pose a threat to the clerk. The trio walks over to the cooler to get beers, but one of them ventures to another aisle to get some chips and cookies.

Kurt tells the clerk, "Put 15 on 4 and to make it quick." The clerk now seems to be aware of his new 'different' customers and is visibly scared. The werewolf who went for snacks looks Kurt's way and begins sniffing wildly in his area, mumbling to himself. "Brimstone… I smell Brimstone." He yells back to his chuckling comrades, "Boys I think we have a masher amongst us." The other two quickly gather to his side.

Kurt turns to them and exposes his guns, "Listen I'm not a masher anymore, I'm retired, and I really don't want any trouble, so why don't you let me leave and no one gets hurt."

They begin licking their lips, and Kurt knows this isn't going to end with them leaving alive. The werewolves begin to change from feral mode to their savage beast transformation of the werewolf. Hair began to cover their faces as their mouths and noses melted into each other and stretched to form a canine mouth. Sharp claws stretch from their nails and you can hear bones crunching and reshaping into the body only made for a beast. They snarl at him and then pounce. When the first one jumps, Kurt fires into the chest, knocking the beast back. He knows that isn't enough to kill him. The other two decide to attack from both sides of Kurt. Kurt knows their plan and surmises that it won't work in a small store like this one. He wastes no bullets on these two as they charge and run into another as Kurt barrel rolls to the left out the way.

The original attacker gets back up with his wounds healing on the spot, he screams, "Fool! It'll take more than that to kill

me!" Kurt says, "Okay." Kurt charges him and knocks him into a freezer. The werewolf throws him off into the row of chips and snacks. He gets up to pounce on Kurt again, but this time, Kurt fires one good shot right between his eyes—instantly killing him. The other two see their mate changing back and lying lifeless on the floor. Kurt points his guns at both of them and says, "Get going before you end up like him." They look at each other, then scamper out the door. Kurt gets up, dusts off, then walks to the counter to pay, but the clerk says, "It's on the house." Kurt shakes his head, grabs his things and heads back on the road.

*****

A man walks into his office and sits down in a large red seat. He is a short, pudgy looking male, balding, with a wide face but narrow nose. He is wearing a poorly tailored suit, and he looks exhausted after his previous meeting. His intercom system is turned on as his secretary, Desi, alerts him, "Mr. Thompson, there's a Mr. Vexor on line one." Richard Thompson voice tremors back, "Thhhhank you Desi, please uh... hold all my calls while I take this."

He answers the phone, "Lord Vexor how can I be of service to you?"

In his sly, yet disarming voice, Vexor replies, "Richard, how can you be of service to me? Well for starters, I need you to stop being (so) useless."

"Whatever you need from me, lord."

Vexor screams, "STOP BEING SO USELESS. TWO NIGHTS AGO, THE SAME MAN YOU TOLD ME WAS NO LONGER A PROBLEM KILLED 3 VAMPIRES OUTSIDE OF NEW MEXICO!"

Richard attempts to speak but is cut off, "Kurt Danger should be DEAD!!! But he isn't and that's because your bureau can't handle an old man, let alone find the little girl I sent you after months ago."

"We may have found the whereabouts of the girl and her grandfather and I'm sending my best agents in the field to apprehend him as we speak."

Vexor laughs hysterically, "Apprehend? Apprehend?! I WANT HIM DEAD! But don't worry about that I'm going to personally make sure he has nowhere to run, and nowhere to hide. As for the girl... good job (I guess) send me the coordinates and I'll have my men handle it."

"Yes, my lord."

Vexor laughs and says, "You know, I helped you become the head of that bullshit bureau, and you were useful for a time, but maybe your usefulness has run out?" Richard hears the dial tone. Shaken to his core, he knows he must do something big to get back in the good graces of Vexor. He presses his intercom system, "Desi... get me Daniels."

# Chapter Two

# ENTER BAXTER WORDSWORTH

Sitting in a diner is a man with a prominent afro, goatee, aviator sunglasses, and an army jacket that conceals his weaponry. He is eating a stack of pancakes and drinking a glass of OJ. The man is Baxter Wordsworth. Two grotesque men walk into the diner, gigantic in their size and stature. They smell and look greenish yet pale with their skin color. They're Mutants, deformed by toxic waste and chemicals. These men–Bobby Rae and his younger brother Eddy Rae–have been tormenting this diner and its patrons for about a year. Now customers are few and far between. The employees are also afraid of these brothers but with no support from local police and no one left to fight back for them, they just take the abuse of the unruly mutants.

The Mutants walk up to the counter and start banging on the table knocking over Baxter's juice. They turn to him and say, "Well damn look what we have gone an did brother we spilled his wittle juice." They continue banging and Eddy Rae says, "You better hurry up with our meal Bitch or this time when we trash this place nobody will recognize it." They laugh hysterically. Baxter sees the young lady in the back terrified. He spoke up,

"Listen here you butt face morons, I don't think they feel like serving you assholes today, so how's about you leave before it's too late to leave." The brothers smile and without hesitation they both grab Baxter and toss him out of the diner through the window.

Baxter shakes off the glass and looks up at his two approaching victims. When they reach him, but before they can say anything, he pulls out a stun gun called the Bolt and fires it upon both assailants. Hit with over 100,000 volts of electricity, the two mutants are tossed backwards on their backs. Baxter laughs as they make an attempt to stand, "I guess ya didn't see that coming... shocking wasn't it?" As Bobby Rae begins to rise, Baxter knee lifts him in the face knocking him back to the ground. Eddy Rae now even angrier, grunting, "Who the Hell are you?"

Baxter smiles pulling out his sawed-off shotgun with the name "Baxter" on the side fires and blows his head clean off. He then walks to the Bobby and butts him in the face with the gun pushes him with his boot making him face up (on his back). Baxter pointed at the mutant's testicular area spoke lowly, bending down.

"Now I am going to spare your life so you can tell your other family members to stay the fuck away from this diner, let them know that a bad Black Mother Fucker with an afro protects this particular diner, and if they come near it starting anymore trouble I'll personally come back to rain all black Hell on their asses!!!"

Scared as hell stutters Bobby looks up, "Of course."

Baxter lets him up and he runs away down the road. Baxter walks back into the Diner and drops money for his meal and the window, the waitress shocked smiles and says, "Thank you but the meal is on us". Baxter smiles and begins to walk out when a familiar car pulls up (by the diner) and beeps. He recognizes the driver and gets in smiling and jokingly responds, "Don't ask, just drive."

In the car, Kurt gives Baxter a look that he fully understood. Baxter looks back at him with a 'what' smile on his face. Kurt just continues to drive waiting.

Baxter finally turns to him, "They'd been terrorizing that diner for a while now, so I've been casing the place, figuring out when was the perfect time to take 'em out. Plus, the ugly assholes spilled my Orange juice. You know how I feel about my Orange juice." They both laugh hysterically. Baxter asks Kurt, "What's going on with you though? Still killing monsters even though you're supposed to be retired?"

Kurt smiles and says, "Yep, you have any idea what's wrong with Samson?"

Baxter adjusts the passenger seat and says, "Nope but it was definitely important enough for him to call us to the diner so we will see once we get there."

The duo rides off. When they arrive at their destination, they get out to a deserted parking lot outside of an old worn-down diner which has a broken sign with the missing letters N, and R. Before they can walk in the front doors, they open up to a frantic creature running away from the gunshots from an old man with a sawed-off shotgun, similar to Baxter's, yelling, "And stay out, you scaly piece of shit!"

Kurt and Baxter take a look at the old man standing in the doorway, he turns to them walking back inside, "You two shitheads coming inside or you standing outside all night?" Kurt and Baxter both shake their heads and follow him inside.

The old man turns to a young woman behind the counter and says, "Elizabeth close up shop, we're headed to the fridge." She nods and Baxter smiles her way, she flips him the bird. The three men head through the kitchen doors, turn to a fridge that leads behind another door, and walk toward an elevator. Once in the elevator Baxter asks, "So who's the babe upfront Samson?"

Samson answers him, "That "babe" is Elizabeth Ortiz, a for-mer Scarab Knight, a superb markswoman, a ruthless bounty hunter. Also, she'd kill you if she heard you call her babe."

Kurt changing the subject before Baxter can say something, "Samson what was so urgent?" The elevator doors open, and they step into a vast monster control center. There are comput-ers, monitors, and advanced technology you wouldn't expect

in a basement area of this kind of diner. Samson goes over to a console area and taps his computer twice and a video shows up on screen of a young lady covered in blood and shaking with limbs all around her.

"This is what's urgent, my granddaughter Maria. You remember my daughter was kidnapped by that demon Nareem?"

Kurt nods.

"Well, he cursed her during that kidnapping and passed down his godforsaken blood to my little Maria. She also, unfortunately, got his power of the blood lust; at the first sign of her own blood or bodily harm to herself or those she cares for, she goes into this trance and becomes a murderous rampaging demon. However, with the help of the Scarab Knights I've been able to keep her relaxed and calm—even found a way to keep her from turning randomly. But last week some Vampire bikers tried to attack her and Elizabeth in a parking lot and this was caught on camera. Liz took her to a small sect of the knights to watch her till we can transport her to the Citadel where the Knights can help train her better and keep her safe. With this video gone viral I fear the worst; vampires after her, the bureau after her, and just about any other damn thing that wants her in some way or for some reason. So, I need you and Baxter to pick her up and help get her safely to the Citadel."

Kurt begins to shake his head, "I'm not a babysitter Samson, Baxter is more than capable of taking care of the girl than me..."

Samson shouts, "You're doing it, both of you, that's final no discussion. Need I remind you," turning to Kurt, "I saved your ass too many times to count but that last time I saved your ass you told me you owe me your life. Well I'm collecting on your debt." Kurt is pissed, remembering what he said to the old man last time they were together.

Seeing his pissed off face, Samson walks over to Kurt and puts his hand on his shoulder, "Kurt she's all I have left of Melissa, the last remaining memory I have of my daughter."

Kurt looks him in his eyes and says, "Dammit Sam, okay I'll do it, but this is my last time. After this back to retirement for real this time."

Just then the elevator opens up, Elizabeth walks out dressed in tactical gear ready for a mission.

"Good to hear you agreed, we leave at sundown so go grab a bite to eat and grab whatever ammo and pieces you need." Baxter looks at her and then looks at Kurt then Samson.

"What she mean "we"?" Samson turns to Baxter, "Elizabeth will accompany you two, Maria knows her but not you two, so she'll only come with you if you're with her." He nodded in Elizabeth's' direction.

Kurt concerned, "What about you, old timer?"

Samson looks... "What about me?"

"What happens if Vexor sends his vampires here after you, who's protecting you?" Samson laughs and opens his arms wide, "I don't need protection Kurt, I have the Fridge. You'll need Elizabeth to get you in the Citadel. Without her they'll kill you and Wordsworth. Besides even if they breach the Fridge,

I still can handle myself." Elizabeth smiles, so does Kurt. Kurt grabs a duffle bag and walks towards the gun locker.

"Alright whatever you want it's your decision Sam. Baxter, I'm going shopping, you need anything?"

Baxter's stomach growls, "Nah I'll be over in a minute, I'm going to grab a bite to eat."

Baxter walks into the makeshift kitchen area, seemingly constructed by scrapes of other appliances, and begins looking in the fridge. Samson walks in behind him and speaks quietly, "I don't know if Kurt is in trouble or not what I do know is your mission. So, make sure he and my granddaughter stay alive. Understood?" Baxter closes the fridge, and stares at him on confirmation. They both nod. Samson walks out saying, "There's tuna for sandwiches on the third shelf." Baxter goes back to looking for food.

Kurt is in the weapons cache looking for what he needs. He adds a couple of handguns, a shotgun, a couple of grenades and a ton of ammo both regular and hellfire bullets to his duffle. Elizabeth watches him from the door.

"Is there some reason you're watching me?"

Elizabeth walks in and Kurt turns around, "He's dying you know; he didn't tell you cause you're so close. I figured you needed to know why this is important to him. It's his dying wish, see that the girl is safe." Kurt stands there shocked his mentor and friend is dying and he can do nothing about it.

He looks down, "What is it? Cancer?"

Elizabeth nods. "Stage four."

"Fuck!"

"So, we have to make sure we don't fail him. No matter what happens we get the girl to the Citadel."

She begins to walk away when Kurt interrupts her, "What happens if the girl goes Blood Lust on us?"

Elizabeth looks down, "Let's hope you do what's right." She looks at him with uncertainty as she walks away.

They end up outside beside Kurt's' car. Baxter calls out "Shotgun!" but Elizabeth gets in the passenger seat disregarding him. Baxter looks at her and says, "Look, you're new to how me and Kurt do things. But I called shotgun."

"Nice, get in the back seat." Baxter looks at Kurt.

Kurt shouts, "Just get in the back Wordsworth." Baxter gets in the back begrudgingly. Samson walks over to the driver side window and leans down, "Be careful Kurt, and if you get in trouble, I know Liz and Bax have your back trust 'em". Kurt nods.

Elizabeth smiles and reassures, "Okay Sam till the next time."

The car pulls off down the road. Unbeknownst to the passengers, something watches them from above and its vision is seen by a dangerous presence. A black hawk circles the diner and looks hard at Samson. It screeches and Samson looks up, then hurries inside. The hawk's eyes are mentally connected to a Warlock named Tarok who controls many beasts eyes around the world. Tarok has found Samson and Kurt Danger for his master, Vexor, the self-proclaimed Prince of all vampires. He

walks into a large extravagant room with hints of crimson red everywhere with one bed draped in velvet shrouds and cloths in the middle. He stands in front of a large black desk adorned with crimson demonic faces and bones.

Vexor walks out of another room which seems to be the bathroom, he's draped in crimson and gold robes. His striking red eyes, pitch black hair, and model type looks match his confident demeanor.

"What did you find?"

Tarok bows, "I've spotted Samson, the girl wasn't with him, but he was accompanied by a woman, a Black man with an afro and... Kurt Danger."

Vexor fills the room with his manic laughter, "It must be my birthday! Well... well... well. Okay Tarok send the hawk to follow wherever Danger goes and give his whereabouts to the nearest pack. As for Samson, get my team together. I'm going to pay him a personal visit."

Tarok looks shocked, "Master, you are going out for this?"

Vexor snaps his fingers and two pale redheaded women come walking in naked with his change of clothes and they disrobe him and clothe him right there looking directly at Tarok. "If you want to make sure a person gets the message, the best way is to deliver the message yourself."

*****

A man walks up a flight of stairs to his apartment building towards his apartment. He gets to his front door and notices

that the welcome mat has been shifted by someone who recently stepped on it. He grabbed his firearm and opened his door with his keys, then he stepped in cautiously taking each step while listening for his uninvited guest. He steps in with his firearm drawn at a man drinking a beer from his fridge.

"Hey Chuck. Figured I'd grab a beer for both of us. Put that gun down, let's chat, I got a really big gig for us." It's Daniels, the partner of Charles Lucia whose apartment was just broken into. Daniels is a small blond man with an intricate set of skills for tracking, he has a pinch in his nose possibly from his former brawling days. His eyes are naturally green, and it just adds to his mystique. His sarcasm and confidence have a tendency to piss off his partner, Charles Lucia A.K.A Bad Luck Chuck. Charles Lucia is an ex-navy seal turned bounty hunter who now takes paid gigs to pay for his ultimate freedom but that's another story for another day. The two men sit down and begin to discuss this lucrative job that will apparently be worth Chuck's time.

*****

In a deep wooded area not too far from Kurt and his team, a wolf walks into a camping ground and lowers its head in a bowing motion to the inhabitants of the camp—Harden's pack. The wolf exchanges information about a car carrying Kurt Danger. Harden the pack leader turns to his pack hunters, "Go avenge your brother, bring me his head!!!" The pack howls back in unison.

# Chapter Three
# STORM'S COMING

"The air is thick, and my knee is killing me." Kurt says out loud.

Baxter immediately says, "Uh oh... that's not good."

Elizabeth asks, "What's not good?"

Baxter replies, "If his knee is hurting and the air is thick, that can mean only one thing."

Elizabeth asks, "What?"

Kurt answers, "It means a storm coming."

Samson is eating a bowl of fruity pebbles at his desk, his shotgun on the table, his sidearm at his side and a solar grenade sits by his container of (warming) almond milk. He notices the alarm going off, he knows the intruders have made it pass the diner defenses, not all of them but enough. He knows the elevator will keep them out, they need the password and how could they... he hears the elevator coming down. He grabs his shotgun and gets in position. Once the elevator arrives, he knows this might be his last minutes of life but if he's going to die, he's going out with a bang.

Just then the elevator doors bust open and Samson began firing into the cloud of smoke emerging. The vampires began to quickly come out moving like acrobats trying to surround him. He switches to his pistols and clips two down, while keeping eyes on his surrounding enemies circling him, jumping and climbing all over the room. One of the vampires charges at him and gets shot in mid-air right in the face. Samson goes back to his sawed-off shotgun and takes down 3 more, then grabs his dagger and launches one right in the heart of the next one creeping behind him.

Then an angry voice emerging from the elevator screams, "Enough!" The vampires stop in place. Samson (takes the time to) surveys the room and sees ten vampires left, he grabs his solar grenade and lifts latch to arm it unbeknownst to his attackers. Then the unknown voice begins laughing, "Damn Samson you really are one killer old bastard, I mean fuck I knew you wouldn't go down easy but damn I definitely didn't think your old ass would kill so many of my men. I knew visiting you personally would be fun." The man walks through smoke, wearing an all-black suit with a crimson tie.

He smiles and when Samson notices whom his new guest is, he immediately shoots at Vexor who dodges runs up and

smacks Samson down. Raising his foot sends him (flying) across the room. On him again before he can move. "When you killed my brother, you were in your prime and still you needed that Asshole Danger to help you out. How's it feel to know you're going to die and the little girl will be mine?" Samson laughs coughing up blood. Vexor is confused as he orders two of his minions to lift Samson up and pin him against the wall.

Another Vampire near the console confirms loudly, "Found the location my lord."

Vexor laughs and Samson laughs harder. Vexor screams at him, "What's so damn funny, you old son of a bitch? Can't you see the girl is as good as dead?"

Samson spits blood in Vexor's face, "Well Vexor, you're still as stupid as you look. For someone hundreds of years old, you just get dumber with age."

He then takes his hidden grenade out of his pocket and releases button, Vexor sees this and says, "Fuck me...." He uses his speed to move towards the exit, but the solar grenade goes off engulfing the entire room in a solar flare, vaporizing all the vampires in the room. Samson collapses.

*****

Rain is pouring out the sky, lightning is flashing, and thunder is roaring. The car occupied by the trio drives along through this rough storm. Elizabeth breaks the silence, "Silence from Kurt is not surprising but you Baxter that's a shocker."

Baxter ignores her leaning up alert and says, "Hey Kurt, you smell that?" Kurt's eyes stare out onto the empty road, he smells a scent that is undeniable. He speeds the car up.

Elizabeth asks, "Is there something I'm missing?"

Just then something on all fours jumps out into the road and Kurt runs it over, the entire car shakes under them and she gasps, "Was that what I think that was?"

Kurt nods, "We're being tracked, werewolves a whole pack. Wet dog is a familiar smell. It's all around us. Baxter get ready this is about…" Just then the car is rammed from the left by a large werewolf and as everyone is trying to recover, it's rammed on the right. A larger werewolf looks right into the driver's window. Kurt knows exactly whose pack this is and he knows they have to get away fast because they're out for blood. Kurt steps on the gas. Elizabeth grabs her gun. Just then another werewolf jumps out on the road, this time he jumps on Kurt's hood and begins to swing violently but Elizabeth shoots through the windshield right between the beast's eyes killing it.

Kurt turns to her angrily, "Did you just shoot my window?"

She shrugs, "I'll pay for the damages if we make it out alive, but until we do… Shut up and DRIVE!" Baxter chuckles and Kurt gives him a look that immediately shuts him up. The bigger werewolf is catching up again about to ram them again. He charges in for the ram and Kurt screams out, "GRAB THE WHEEL!" Kurt lets go of the wheel and pulls out his sawed-off shotgun. He takes down the beast as it leaps, blasting its muzzle right off—not killing him but definitely knocking him

back while Elizabeth grabbed the wheel. Kurt takes back the wheel and they speed away from the pack for now.

*****

Samson crawls to his extra pistol on the desk, he grabs it but is immediately knocked down by Vexor again. Vexor's face is half burnt but is, unfortunately, repairing rapidly. He stands over menacingly of the knocked down Samson, he kicks him hard in the ribs breaking two of his ribs in the process. He grabs Samson and lifts him up, then throws him into a monitor. Seeing a crumbled Samson Vexors hysterical laughter fills the room, he picks up Samson by his throat. Samson has broken ribs and is bleeding internally but the Asshole that helped in his daughter's death is laughing in his face. Samson spits in his face, making the laughter stop abruptly. Vexor face contorts in a grimace as he chokeslams Samson to the floor and begins tightening his fingers. Samson struggles but he can't get loose from his grip.

Vexor continues to choke him whispering to him as the air leaves him, "The little girl is mine, I'm going to use her as my catalyst to my Vampire Armageddon. I'm going to kill Kurt Danger just like I'm killing you, you worthless old piece of shit." Samson stares into the eyes of his murderer and knows this is the end. On his last breath Vexor gets up and fixes his attire, wipes the blood off his face with his handkerchief and walks out. He gets outside, lights a cigarette as a car pulls up and a woman comes out and opens his door. He gets in and picks up his tablet to begin looking at the location of the young girl.

Vexor smiles, "Tell echo team to go to the coordinates I just sent them and retrieve the girl for me and meet me at the office."

*****

Driving down the road, Kurt and company know they barely made it out alive from their recent attack. Kurt knows that pack is still on their scent and they haven't escaped—not by a long shot.

Baxter laughs, "Shit I know we just almost died but damn awkward silence isn't going to help us."

Elizabeth confused, "Yeah Kurt we couldn't have escaped them so easily, right?"

Kurt replies, "No they have our scent they're still on our tails."

Elizabeth turns to him alarmed, "Kurt we can't lead them where we're headed. We'll risk something happening to the girl."

"Okay so we have to stop and take these wolves on our tail out. I hope you're ready for this?"

Elizabeth cocks back her gun, looks over at him and says, "Been ready." Baxter leans up and begins smiling from ear to ear. Further down the road they pull over and into an embankment wooded area and they prepare for the pack. Then wait.

They didn't have to wait long. The werewolves start sniffing closer, one of the pack members started down the dirt hill toward the group. He has their scent and begins walking over, he sees a cigar lit and he rushes toward it--SNAP! His leg is snapped in the bear trap they set, he howls out but is quickly

silenced by an arrow between the eyes. The others come down following the sound (of their pack member)

"Danger come out and finish this you bastard!" screams the largest one in the pack. Another werewolf close whimpers as he is shot by a sniper right through the eyes.

Kurt screams out in warning, "That's two leaving you four. Believe me if this is about your pack member the other day, I'm about to give you the same ultimatum. Leave now or don't leave at all and add to the body count of your pack."

The largest one howls back in anger, "Fuck you Danger!" A grenade rolls over to them, one of them picks it up to sniff it but before his leader can notice it explodes. Kurt, Baxter, and Elizabeth walk out to the charred mutilated bodies and begin shooting the remaining werewolves in the head right between the eyes. Kurt walks over to the leader as he crawls away with one arm whimpering Kurt kicks him over on his back and looks him in the eye, "These deaths are on you not me." He fires the final shot. The group heads back to the car and gets back on the road.

Soon they arrive at the destination, an abandoned church. Elizabeth gets out the car first and walks up to a decrepit tree.

Baxter asks Kurt, "What is she doing?"

Pulling out a bejeweled Knife with a gold Scarab on the hilt. She then stabs the tree and the tree glows informing the Scarab knights inside that she has arrived. Kurt and Baxter are stunned, "Well there's something you don't see every day." whispers Baxter.

Elizabeth calls to them, "You two can get out now, if they're here they now know it's me. Just then, the doors open and a young dark red-haired girl dressed in oversized garments comes running out towards Elizabeth shouting, "You're back!!!" She embraces Elizabeth with the tightest hug ever. Kurt and Baxter step out the car and Maria instantly looks their way and Elizabeth reassures, "That's your pop pop's friends they're here to help me keep the bad people away from you." Just then one of Scarab knights comes out and gestures to the crew to step inside.

Elizabeth says to everyone, "Let's get out of the cold and go inside. We will speak further inside." Once inside the Scarab knights greet Elizabeth and the others, "Welcome back Liz, thanks to our past pharaohs for your protection. Welcome to your friends as well, may the pharaohs' protection rise and set upon you both." She nods towards them.

Elizabeth, relieved, says, "Thank you Forah, and Kri for your protection of Maria. This is Kurt Danger and his friend Baxter Wordsworth. They were handpicked by Samson to accompany me on my mission. Have there been any other episodes since the last?" Forah softly, "Thankfully no but Maria has been anxiously awaiting your return." Maria smiles at Liz.

Kurt wonders, "How secure is that protection spell you have on the church?"

Kri smiles, "Familiar with the arts, are you? I'd expect nothing less from someone associated with Samson. That spell is used to keep anyone not invited inside the church by a Scarab knight to cross the threshold. That is why the Scarab dagger

was used as a key to alert us that Liz has returned to us. Inside these doors we are all safe."

Baxter laughs, "As long as we stay in here, but unfortunately we will need to leave to take the girl to the Citadel." Maria is shocked, she believed it was all over.

"What! I thought I was going back home to Grandpa, why do I have to be locked away? I didn't do anything wrong!"

Elizabeth looks scornful in Baxter's direction turning to Maria, "Listen honey we need to take you to my elders so they can help you. The people after you won't stop till they find you. But with the Elders you'll be safe, and they can help you with your episodes."

Maria screams out, "I don't care, I don't need help, there's nothing wrong with me. I thought you were my friend Lizzy but you're just like everyone else you want to lock me away. I'M NOT GOING!!!" She runs out the church.

"Maria, come back!" screams out Elizabeth. "Damn Baxter your mouth never shuts does it?" Elizabeth shouted back at Baxter as she follows Maria. Before Baxter can answer they hear Maria scream, she is in trouble. The group follows Elizabeth and runs out to her aid and then see 150 or more Vampires surrounding Maria.

Kurt sarcastically mumbles as he loads his gun, "Well isn't that just convenient."

At Manny's Auto Repair shop, Manny is working on a car when three men walk into his shop. These men are wearing all black tactical gear and one of them has on shades and a visible

scar above and below his left eye. The other two are similar size to each other but one is blonde looking like a model type guy, the other is half head with tats all over his head. They are Mashers, the tall one with shades clears his throat getting Manny's attention, "I'm going to keep this short and sweet where was Kurt Danger heading and please both our sakes don't tell me you don't know him because that would anger me and you do not want to make me angry one bit."

Manny starts to stutter, and he is picked up by the larger man, "Where did he say he was going?"

Manny stammers, "To see an old friend."

Seconds later, the trio get back into an all-black Hummer and the leader of this group opens a laptop and begins to type, the computer soon chimes. "Bingo got him. Buckle in boys we are making a stop at an old friend's place a few miles up the road." The other two laugh as the black Hummer pulls off.

# Chapter Four

# LUCK IS FOR SUCKERS

One of the vampires walks forward and says, "We're already taking the girl, but killing the legendary Kurt Danger would be a bonus." He begins laughing, until he is shot down and turned into ashes by a bullet from Kurt. As the other vampires are shocked Baxter begins shooting the other ones, Elizabeth calls out to Maria, "Maria! Run to me, hun!"

She begins to back track towards Elizabeth until she is knocked down by a charging Vampire. Maria's head hits the ground hard and she is slightly stunned. Kurt sees this and screams out to Baxter, "Cover me!"

Kurt runs towards her dropping vampires as they get closer, as Baxter drops any other vampires he doesn't kill. Forah has a golden staff and charges in towards the girl along with Elizabeth. She drops one by one, Forah uses his staff to pole vault towards Maria landing and striking vampires back with his impressive martial art skills. Each one he knocks down, he switches his staff to a spear and stabs them through the heart, dusting them. Baxter continues to shoot covering Kurt and Liz.  Kurt and Liz finally reach the girl and stand back to back and begin shooting the other vampires down covering the girl. Kurt stops to pick up the girl and then Maria wakes up with different eyes.

Maria eyes glow red with fury at him, she pops up from his arms and runs with lightning speed towards another Vampire pouncing on him and ripping his neck out with her new protruded sharp fangs, Kurt is shocked and caught off guard by another Vampire who takes him down. Elizabeth says, "Forah we have a problem!" Forah turns to see Maria charging another Vampire then being bludgeoned to death by her fist. Taking his eyes off his attackers for the split second is a costly mistake as he is slashed on the back by one vampire and the other tackles him down slashing his face before biting into the side of his throat and tearing it out. Kri and Elizabeth scream out in shock. Baxter shoots the Vampire on top of Kurt then the one on top of the slain Forah. Kurt nods to him and turns to find Maria snapping the arm off another Vampire then flipping over him and kicking his head through the ground.

Kurt yells to Elizabeth, "How do we stop her? We need to get out of here!"

"We have to knock her out again."

Kurt nods, "Got it!" He runs over to her and seeing him she changes direction to charge him. "Oh shit. Okay that's it, come to me dear."

When she jumps in the air he dodges (pick a direction) and gun butts her hard on the back of the head knocking her out then shooting three more Vampires. He quickly grabs her and runs towards the car.

"Let's go NOW!!" They all head towards the car. Kri runs over to the fallen body of his brother where he is taken down by another Vampire. Elizabeth turns to help him, but Kurt screams back at her, "There's no time Liz come on now!"

They rush into the car and Kurt drops Maria in the back and quickly tosses a flash solar grenade out the window and it explodes taking a few out and blinding the others. The car peels off and they barely make it out alive.

*****

Chuck and Daniels are driving down a road, Daniels in the drivers' seat while Chuck reads up on the target. He flips through the file and stops on a particular page.

"This guy seems like he truly believes he's killing monsters."

Daniels responds, "Most people believe they're the hero of their own story".

Chuck flips to one page and sees something that baffles him, "This guy wasn't always some vigilante, he worked for the same people who hired us. Now they want him dead or

alive. Daniels, this situation smells like bullshit." Looking at Daniels concerned.

Daniels looks back and says, "But the pay isn't, so let's just take this huge payday and worry about our moral compasses later. Actually, let's worry about our stomachs for now." They both laugh and continue to drive.

*****

Snipes and his team of Mashers arrive at the diner which was Samson's base. Samson used to work for the Mashers and he's a legend and was also Snipes and Kurt's mentor. He knew Kurt was going to go to find Samson. He still doesn't understand why they have been sent after Kurt, but orders are orders. They walk in the Diner and see the place trashed and the kitchen door is hanging off the hinges. He and his team head down the elevator. When the doors open, he sees what confirms his suspicions.

"Someone came and attacked this place hard and fast. The old man gave them quite the battle, but they eventually got the best of him."

He sees his old mentor bloodied and dead, and he grits his teeth to hold back tears. He turns and calls his boss, "Wherever Danger is, there seems to be someone also after him cause they already took out former Masher Samson. Sir, we might need to head back in and get more information." He nods with a frown on his face. "Understood Sir." He puts his phone back in his pocket.

He turns back and says to his team, "We are being called back in."

They walk out and pile in the truck and the hummer peels off down the road.

*****

Vexor is in his office reading a Time magazine. Dorian Gray—Billionaire Playboy of the Year is on the cover. Vexor is interrupted by Tarok walking in.

"Lord Vexor, I beg your pardon I bring visions of the (groups) last encounter with Kurt Danger."

Vexor smiles, puts down his magazine and motions to Tarok to proceed. Tarok walks over to this basin with a smoky liquid rising out of it. He cries a single tear inside the liquid and it ignites blue flames. Rising into images in the air the battle is shown to Vexor. Vexor sees the girls' powers and is very intrigued even more so than before. The visions continue until the bright light from the solar flare grenade Kurt throws blinds the birds' sight. The visions end, Vexor laughs at the scene playing. Tarok is confused.

"Lord Vexor we lost sight of where they're headed next."

Vexor unperplexed says, "Her powers are magnificent, she is every bit of the demon my brother was. The girl will be my ticket to becoming the most powerful Vampire ever." He turns to Tarok and says, "Get out the word to every vampire, demon, werewolf, mutant and creature of the night. Tell them whomever and whatever brings me the head of Kurt Danger and the little girl he has with him alive, I, Vexor, Prince of all

vampires will give them riches beyond their wildest dreams and much, much more." He resumes laughing returning to his magazine.

Kurt looks in the back seat at Baxter who is sitting with the girl concerned.

"How's the girl Baxter?"

"Still knocked out."

Elizabeth sitting in the passenger seat is still distraught over the deaths of her fellow Scarab Knights (and friends), she looks at Maria and begins to only see her in blood lust.

Kurt screams out to her to snap her out of it. "Listen Liz, we need to figure out what's our next move. What I saw back there, that changes things. Maria isn't going to be as easily cured as you think."

Elizabeth snaps out of it and turns to him, "The plan remains the same Kurt. We deliver Maria to the Knights at the Citadel and they'll handle the rest."

Kurt looks at her slightly baffled by her response, "That thing inside of her ripped limbs off of grown men twice her size and then she came after me. I almost..."

"Almost what Kurt? Almost what? Pulled the goddamn trigger like you were told to do? Well let's hope it doesn't come to that!"

Just then Maria starts to stir, Baxter whispers, "Quit it you two the girl is starting to wake." They each turn around at Maria's eyes opening. Maria looks at each of them with her brown eyes and whispered, "It happened again didn't it?" Her head hung.

Elizabeth smiles at her, her face softening, "It's okay hun we are safe (for) now and I'm going to make sure you make it to the Citadel so you can be safe." Maria's stomach growls loudly, Baxter laughs and says, "Sounds like someone is in need of pancakes. You want breakfast?"

Maria smiles, "Yes sir. Can we Liz?"

Kurt looks over at Liz, "There's a diner up the road next exit."

She looks back and forth between Maria and Kurt, "Okay let's eat."

Maria squeals out with excitement. "Yes!"

Chuck and Daniels arrive at Cherry's Diner and grab a table in the back. Cherry's place is patterned after a traditional diner in the sixties and seventies, with ruby red seats for cushions, stools, booths and a jukebox. Cherry's place is usually busy around 7am but today its only patrons are Chuck and Daniels, a small family of three, two truckers and some strange looking guys dressed in all black with tons of piercings and tattoos. Chuck and Daniels are served their coffee while they await their ordered platters. Chuck can't help but stare at the guys in the back. Something is odd about them. Just then in comes (to their luck) Elizabeth, Baxter with Maria followed lastly by Kurt. Chuck and Daniels look at each other, they can't believe it their bounty just walked right into the Diner.

 Chuck says to Daniels, "Okay what an unlucky day for Kurt Danger."

Daniels laughs, "Well lucky day for you and me, partner. So, we nab him after breakfast when he leaves to deal with less commotion."

Chuck nods while sipping his coffee in agreement, "What about the others?"

Daniels looks at the foursome as they're seated in a booth towards the back right, "Shock treatment for Afro man, the lady seems tough though she might need knocking out, and the girl tranq dart and it's night, night, sleep tight." Chuck nods in agreement as their order arrives.

When Chuck and Daniels stepped in the diner, they noticed five individuals dressed in all black, these individuals are called the Night Stalkers. Practitioners of dark magic, they have no magical bloodlines, nor do they serve any higher or darker purpose; in fact, Kurt would say they're just a group of dickheads who like to use magic to cause trouble wherever they go. This morning they just happened to have received a message regarding Kurt Danger and these particular Dickheads are looking to cash in on that bounty. They noticed Chuck and Chuck noticed them but neither party knows who or what the other's motives are so for now they continue to eat their breakfast and plot on how they can each get this bounty. Just then the baldheaded one in the group whose name is Stitch notices Chuck looking at him, "Why is this guy staring at me?"

The smaller male, named Verb, has an all-white Mohawk. Looking in Chuck's direction he grimaces, "Well he's ugly as fuck. Maybe he likes ya Stitch?"

Stitch is about to smack Verb when someone walks in and steals his attention away, "Well, well, fellas it's our lucky day, cause our ticket to the top just walked in to eat."

Verb says, "Well I'll be damned Kurt Danger gift wrapped, along with the little girl. It is our lucky Day."

Stitch makes a plan, "We wait till he's finished and then we take him down with no hesitation." Kurt and crew are seated 3 booths down from them. They can wait.

Arriving at Cherry's Diner, Kurt is last through the door and begins to scope out the room. A small family of three that are just getting up to leave, two truckers who seemed to be relaxing, the two by the counter are some sort of undercover cops, he can tell by gun holster imprints, and then there's those clowns over there. Sitting at a table in the back of the Diner sits a group of Night Stalkers, bootleg sorcerers with limited magical skills and the capacity to attract large quantities of idiots to join their group. These particular idiots don't look dangerous, but they do look like they could be annoying. His group is seated in a booth not too far from the idiots.

As they're seated a waitress named Rosie comes to take their orders, "Hey Baxter long time no see hun. What you doing 'round these parts?"

Baxter smiles, "Well Rosie my friends and I are taking my niece out for her Birthday pancakes, and she has never had your Famous Cherry Cakes Special." Baxter winks at everyone Maria winks back.

Rosie has a huge smile on her face and says, "Well cutie pie what's your name? And how old are you today?" Maria is in on the whole thing, much to the enjoyment of Baxter, "Maria is my name and Ma'am I'm 10yrs old."

Rosie smiles and replies, "Well little Maria, one order of the Cherry Cakes Special coming up. The usual for you Baxter?"

"Certainly Rosie."

Rosie turns to Kurt and Liz, "Coffee Black shot of espresso three sugars for Kurt, and you my dear?" Kurt nods.

Elizabeth says, "I'll have eggs scrambled with cheese and sausage links, with a regular tea, no sugar."

Rosie takes down their orders and makes her way to the back, Baxter pleased smiles at Maria, "This girl's a natural."

Maria smiles back and shrugs, "Girls' gotta do what a girls' gotta do for the pancakes." This breaks everyone out into laughter. A couple of minutes pass, and the orders are brought out to the crew. As Baxter teaches his new protégé the fine arts of eating a Cherry Cakes Special, Liz gets up to go to the bathroom. When Liz passes the table occupied by the group of Night Stalkers, she notices their dark aura. Upon returning from the bathroom Liz asks can she speak with Kurt for a second.

Kurt and Liz walk over to a corner near restrooms, "That group in the back, I felt a bad aura coming from their table, I think they practice the dark arts."

"You're good cause they're bootleg sorcerers, part of a cult called the Night Stalkers." says Kurt.

Liz is worried, "Well they felt way stronger than they look… at least one of them isn't a second-rate magic user."

Kurt nods agreeing, "Right well let's wrap this up and get back on the road, because just like you I'm sensing something bad is about to happen." Liz agrees and they both head back to the table.

As they head back to the table, a waitress named Sara is carrying drinks for the Night Stalkers when one of them decides to make her trip using a spell. She falls and the drinks spill on Stitch angering him and he gets up in a fit of anger shouting, "Enough dicking around." He turns to Kurt and shoots a locking spell on the front door, "Where do you think you're going, Kurt?" He sneers over at Kurt getting ready to tell the others to leave. Now Kurt knows this fight can't be avoided but there are way too many innocent bystanders around that he can't risk them getting hurt.

Baxter stands and pulls out his weapon followed by Liz and Kurt, "Listen up knuckleheads, you want to fight cool I'm all for it but let the people leave, they have nothing to do with this, any grudge you got with me take it up with me." Kurt spoke to the group.

They all begin to laugh, "This ain't about no grudge fool this is about the girl and the bounty on your head. We ain't leaving without the girl and your head on a silver platter." Kurt is confused. What bounty?

Just then Daniels and Chuck pull out their guns and point it towards the Night Stalkers, "I could care less about the girl, but the old guy is me and my partners bounty and we want him alive so that makes you idiots a liability, right Chuck?" Chuck nods and the standoff begins. Chuck yells over at the Night Stalkers, "Now unless you want your heads removed from your bodies, I suggest you back off and leave Kurt to us." Verb is anxious, he is way too riled up to be calm, he looks at Kurt and crew and knows what Kurt is capable of, he looks at the other two guys unsure of who they are, all he knows for sure is he's not trying to get shot. He looks at Stitch and notices him shaking. His mind is made up, he's got to do something. His hands spark with a purple hue of what can only be described as flickering flames, and he mutters some incantation right before a purple fireball shoots from his hands knocking back Kurt Danger into a table. It happened so quick it was almost unseen by normal eyes or untrained eyes. Baxter sees this and without hesitation begins firing shots at Verb, these shots are absorbed by a force field created by the woman of their group called Nickels.

Stitch yells out, "What the flying fuck is your malfunction Verb? Nickels keep their fire off of us while I figure out how to nab the girl." Chuck looks at Kurt's body as it lays there unconscious, and the little girl he knows nothing about begins to scream. "What in the blue hell is going on?" Just then something else he's never seen happens before his eyes. Stitch casts a spell to make the knives and forks glow with the same purple hue and begin flying around everywhere. Everyone begins ducking and dodging cutlery while Liz covers up and tries to console a frightened Maria. Just then one of Knives flies straight into the throat of one of the truckers, then through Rosie and Chuck sees this is getting out of control.

"We need to break that barrier she has up so I can take the tall one out." yells Chuck to his partner, who has a good idea about how to get that done. Daniels notices a fire extinguisher and that it's behind the group, behind the force field created by the woman. She can only protect their front and their stalling with this knife show till he can figure out a way to get to Kurt, Daniels is a master planner, but Chuck is a master marksman. He whispers to Chuck, "See that fire extinguisher?"

"Yeah."

"It's on their blindside behind her force field crap."

Chuck smiles and stands up for a quick ricochet shot off the Diner wall straight into the fire extinguisher. When he shoots this bullet it's a thing of beauty, directly piercing the extinguisher causing it to explode behind the Night Stalkers knocking most of them out in the process. When Verb comes up to Baxter fires a bullet directly into his head followed by Chuck shooting Nickels before she can conjure up any more force fields. This enrages Brick who was Nickels lover. He charges forward a beam of energy and flings it through Daniel's heart, impaling him.

Chuck screams, "Daniels NO!" He fires several shots back at Brick killing him, kneeling next to check on Daniels. He's bleeding from his mouth, the wound in his chest is fatal. Daniels can only say a few words before his final breath. As he whispers them into Chuck's ear, he dies in his arms, pissing Chuck off.

Stitch stirs and the last one of his crew, Ghost is standing there... Stitch screams, "Get us out of here Ghost!" Ghost looks over and disappears with a poof of dust leaving Stitch, "Son of a monkey's bitch!" He turns to see Kurt waking up and Chuck pointing a gun right at him. BLAM! One shot to the kneecap. BLAM!!! Another shot to his right hand, BLAM! Another shot to his testicles. Stitch screams out in pain and agony. Music to Chuck in his rage. Chuck walks up to him and he notices Kurt getting up, "No Kurt don't get up, you stay right where you're at I'm not done with you yet."

Kurt struggles to get up, ignoring Chuck, surveying the damage around the room then he hears faint sirens and knows one of these people called the authorities during the blowout. He knows they have to get going. Chuck, not hearing the sirens, looks down at Stitch, his voice laced with pain, "I know you don't care, but you bastards killed my friend and that means you have to die. Today was your unlucky day." BLAM! Shot right through the face. He turns to see the purple hue on the door disappear and Baxter pointing his gun directly at him now.

"Listen, I don't know who you are, and I'm sorry about your partner but you're not going anywhere with Kurt. So, we are going to walk on out of here--the four of us--grab our car and get the hell away from you. Got it?" Baxter begins signaling to Liz to grab Maria and head for the door. They slowly move towards the door (not taking their eyes off Chuck.). Kurt covers them, standing up and pointing his gun at Chuck.

"Don't know if you hear those sirens but from the looks of things, you're no cop and when they get here, they're taking us all down, so I suggest you get the picture and get gone." With that Kurt opens the door and his group leave the diner. They quickly get in their car and leave heading north.

Chuck stands there for a second watching them, shakes his head and laughs. He drops a hundred dollar bill on the blood splattered counter and grabs his partners' wallet, closing his eyes. He leaves in pursuit of Kurt and crew just before the authorities arrive. This is far from over (as he grips the wheel).

# Chapter Five

# RIDE BLACK BEAUTY RIDE

"What in the world was that?!" Baxter exclaimed. Kurt rubs at his chest as he drives, his chest still hurting from the magician's fireball blast. Liz sits with Maria in the back, Maria who is still shaken up by the whole ordeal sits quietly.

Kurt, ignoring his friend's question, looks in the rearview mirror at them, "How's Maria?"

"She'll be fine, we just need to get as far away from there as possible. Who was that guy?"

Kurt thinks back to the ordeal and sees the face of the man clearly, he whispers his name, "Chuck."

Baxter stares at Kurt for a second, "Those guys looked like Feds, but they weren't. They had a bounty on your head. So did the Assholes with the magic, but they sounded like their bounty included our little friend. I'd stake my life Vexor had something to do with that bounty. But the Chuck guy I have no idea why they're after you Kurt."

Kurt turns to him, "Get on your web and see if you can find anything about a bounty on me and the girl. As far as the Chuck guy, I have a feeling we haven't seen the last of him." He looks in his rearview mirror rubbing his chest again.

An assistant walks quickly down a long hallway. Her steps in her all red pumps can be heard as she makes her way to her master's office. The long red hallway surrounding her is decorated with classic Victorian décor and statuesque sculptures from Transylvania. She turns the corner and scans her eyes in the door. The doors open and she walks into the large office, huge with monitors hanging above, a large mirror on the left wall with a creepy statue of a demon on the top, an even larger desk sits in the middle with her Master, Victor Vexor sitting behind it.

Vexor raises his hand gesturing for her to wait, he is in the middle of a phone call, "Yes, Danger is a nuisance, but he is one we soon will be rid of. We have several plans to deal with him and the girl. Yes, I agree. It will be worth it Master." He hangs up. "This had better be good news Charlotte."

Charlotte walks closer and smiles, "Kurt Danger had a run in with some low rate Darkstalkers, he got away, but he's wounded, and we know which way he's going." Vexor begins

to laugh and gets up, "Well then let's send a welcome party to that location so we can greet him (properly) when he arrives. It'll be a nice surprise party." Charlotte nods and exits calling the necessary people.

Chuck is racing in his car trying to catch up to his bounty, he taps on his tablet when the screen reads "Profile complete." He tells his tablet, "Give me all the info you have on the Bureau of Cryptid and Paranormal Abnormalities. Let's see who our employer really is and why he's after you Mr. Danger." His tablet begins to pull up dozens of files, while Chuck sees visions of his partner's death over and over and begins to drive faster, he must finish this (for Daniels).

*****

Snipes and his crew are traveling down the road when they get distinct information about local law enforcement checking out quite the bloody mess at a Diner not too far from where they are. They take a detour and head on over to investigate this incident.

Kurt and his passengers have pulled off the road into an off beaten area, surrounded by dirt and trees. They drive a little further until Liz whispers, "Park the car here, we're going to walk the rest of the way."

Kurt gives her an "Are you crazy" look on his face, "I'm not just parking Beauty here without a care in the world."

Baxter interjected before Liz could speak. He shook his head at her. "Kurt loves this car."

Liz looks over at Kurt, "It will be safe plus where we are headed the car can't make it, we have to travel on foot. While we're gone, I'll let one of the Scarab knights know where the car is, and they can come put a cloaking spell on it." Kurt still looks angry but parks between some trees and takes the keys out.

"Your people better be able to help the girl." He warns. They begin to walk towards their destination, Kurt doesn't know what it is, but he can't shake the bad feeling he has. They walk through the wooded area, Baxter in the middle holding Maria's hand tightly as they traverse the trail. Elizabeth leading the way with Kurt taking up the rear for protection. The wooded area feels different the further in they go, it smells ancient and feels more mystical.

Elizabeth whispered, "There's an enchantment on this part of the area, if you are a Scarab knight you'll always feel better here, it gives off a sense of healing."

They continue to walk until they arrive at a thick moss and vine covered wall. Elizabeth walks up to the wall and whispers into it making the wall disassemble, as the bricks begin to move around, and the vines and moss melts away revealing a doorway. They walk through to see a church-like structure behind the wall, and a man in black and gold robes standing at the door. The man had a black and gold face with a golden scarab on his headband.

Elizabeth happily shouts, "Eigel! Nassir! So good to see you again cousins." She runs towards the man.

Baxter confusingly laughs out, "Welp Liz has lost it she is seeing two people now." Just then the man at the door splits

down the middle and one man becomes two, Eigel wearing gold looking like a male version of Elizabeth and Nassir dressed in all black identical to his twin. Baxter's mouth, open wide, mumbled, "Magic, I hate magic."

The two men both hug Elizabeth, "It has been too long cousin, but now you are home." Eigel happily spoke as they released from their hug.

Elizabeth smiles, "It has certainly been a long time, but my dear cousin we must get the girl inside. I fear for her life even as we speak. Is your father busy? I must speak with him at once."

Nassir says, "No, he is in his sanctuary, awaiting your arrival. Go to him at once, we will make sure your friends are fed and taken care of."

The large door opens up inward and Elizabeth calls out to Maria, "Come with me Maria and meet my uncle."

Maria looks up at Baxter and warns, "Be safe."

She runs to Elizabeth and they go through the door. The men at the door watch as the door closes. Another Scarab knight comes and welcomes Baxter and Kurt waving them over as he leads them to the kitchen. They are clothed in attire that crosses between a ninja and a priest. Some wear masks over their mouths and headband that features the icon of the Golden Scarab. Others wearing black head wraps and hoods.

*****

As Elizabeth and Maria make their way to the Sanctuary, the meditation room of her uncle, Maria asks "Liz can your Uncle really help me?"

"My uncle is a master of the mystical, if anyone can he can." Maria smiles as they enter the Sanctuary. Maria looks around this large dimly lit room, there are candles everywhere, as well as what seems like hundreds of books on the bookshelves lining the walls. The place seems bigger inside than it did outside, and it had strange markings on the walls. In the middle of a room is what looks to be a fountain with two faucets in the shape of claws. Sand ran from their faucets, the sand seemed to have a never-ending flow. Standing near one of the bookshelves is a long-haired man in a long robe that had the exact same markings etched in all over it. The man was deep in his search for something.

"Have a seat my dear, I almost have the book I'm looking for." The man spoke out without looking up.

"But there aren't any seats Liz."  Looking around for a chair to sit.

The man laughs, "Ah the innocence of youth." He waves his hands backwards and a desk appears with two seats in front of it and a large chair behind it. Maria is shocked as her and Liz have a seat. "Ha, there it is." The man pulls out a thick red book laced in gold trimmings. When he turns, Maria sees the kindest face she's ever seen, he has a long beard to accompany his long hair and glasses with larger lenses and a button nose. This is Elizabeth's uncle Magnus and the Scarab Knights leader. Magnas sits down at the desk. He places the

book down on the table and opens it to the middle of the book. He holds his glasses as he thumbs through the book to a page, "There it is, the answers are always where you least expect it." He marveled out loud.

Elizabeth clears her throat, "Uncle Magnas, this is Maria. The young lady I informed you about. We might be in serious danger becau–"

Magnas cuts her off, "Kurt Danger has arrived with you? He is with the man out of time in the dining area."

Elizabeth is shocked. She shakes her head. "Kurt has helped me get Maria to you, this "man out of time" I'm confused by though only Baxter is with him ..."

Magnas says, "All will be revealed in due time my dear. For now, this beautiful young lady needs food and rest." At that comment, a woman, Magnas turns towards Maria (and smiles), "Maria let Sasha know what you'd like to eat, and drink and she will make sure you get it."

Maria looks at Liz unsure.

"Go with Sasha, Maria. You're safe here. I'll catch up with you soon hun."

Maria walks over to Sasha looking back, "Don't take too long Liz." Walking out with Sasha.

Magnas waits until she's far enough down the hall. Turning to his niece, "I fear removing the curse from her will result in her death."

Elizabeth shouts standing up, "What?! You said you could help her!"

Magnas smiles, "Help her we shall, however, we will help her control it, teach her the way of the Scarab and help her use her curse as a strength rather than a hindrance."

Elizabeth breathes out reassured, "Thank you Uncle." (Relaxing back into the chair.)

*****

Kurt and Baxter are eating in a large cafeteria area, Baxter is scoping out the place and he also has an uneasy feeling about this place. The cafeteria is huge; it has multiple tables with about 6 or 8 chairs to each table. Each table sits a group of Scarab Knights and most of them are engaged in eating and conversation. Baxter notices one in particular staring at him, the man that looks at him has a scar through his eye and a weird look about him. He notices Baxter looking at him and he gets up and walks off. Baxter is officially suspicious and turns to Kurt.

Baxter taps Kurt, "Hey I'm getting that feeling you always talk about, the one where…"

"Where shit doesn't feel right, and it feels like something bad is about to go down." Kurt finishes.

Baxter nods, "Exactly. That's the feeling I'm getting now. Something feels odd like there's a false sense of security here."

Just then a woman sitting next to them overheard reassures them, "You two are safe here, no one can come through those walls without the proper spell."

Kurt says, "But if someone did want in here all it takes is the proper motivation." Looking around the room alert.

Magnas holds Elizabeth's hand looking at her in the eyes, "Things aren't the same without you here, your training is still incomplete, and your family is incomplete."

Elizabeth smiles, "Uncle Magnas you know this isn't my journey. I may have been born in the sect, but my calling is more than a mystic reading prophecies, and awaiting some dark Lord's Armageddon. I do real good out there with Samson, saving people from real threats."

Magnas nods, "We all must walk in our own path. But I feel more training in the arts of the Scarab wouldn't hurt." Looking at a bookshelf in the corner.

Near the wall on the outskirts of the Citadel walks the scared eyed man he touches the wall whispering "HectooFahtoo," and the wall begins to open up revealing Vexor and a small mob of Werewolves and Vampires at his side. The man kneels down in front of Vexor, "Master he is here with the girl the doors are guarded by the twin mages and their invisible three. Once they are alerted there will be more sent to their aid. Time is of the essence."

Vexor unperturbed smiles down menacingly, "Go cause havoc, while me and Fahban go grab the girl. Oh, and leave one of your doorways open for my friend Stonehenge." The mob of monsters begin running frantically towards the front gate from the side. While a massive grey skinned troll with the texture of granite, follows slowly behind them.

Inside, Kurt is uneasy and is wondering what's taking Liz so long, he taps Baxter and Baxter turns to him, "Something feels bad, I think we need to grab the girl and leave now."

Baxter agrees with him standing up, "This place seems like it's not as safe as they think."

Kurt turns back towards the tent area where Elizabeth headed with the girl, "I'm going to get the girls and then I think we need to get out of dodge." Kurt gets up from his table, but a scent hits him and he begins to sniff in the air; he looks towards the entrance then at Baxter, "Get Liz and the girl now!" Pulling out his weapons aiming at the entrance.

Baxter turns to Kurt, "Werewolves." He races over to where Elizabeth and Maria are supposed to be.

At the entrance to the church Eigel and Nassir stand guard in their united form. He senses darkness and immediately turns toward the direction he senses the trouble, "Invisible Three to my side. We are under attack."

Just then three silhouettes jump from the rooftop of the Church. As they land their true forms emerge from the reflective camouflage that allowed them to be invisible to reveal three Scarab Knight guards adorned in gold and black samurai like armor with Scarab emblems on the chest plates and the head garb of a ninja covering their faces. As they position, turning

the corner is an onslaught of twenty Vampires and Werewolves dressed in all black charging the defenders of the gate.

The twins united form speaks loud and clear, "I do not know who betrayed us by granting you access to this Sanctuary but on this day, you will not enter this sacred place." He grabs his horn and blows alerting the knights. Then as the first eager wolf lunges toward them he splits the beast into two and slices it's head off while his brother slams a knife deep between the eyes of the fallen head fully severing it from its life. (Then they charge the oncoming mob.)

Inside the horn is heard and everyone stands (full) alert. In the sanctuary tent Liz turns towards the entrance and back towards her Uncle suddenly frantic, "Where did she take Maria?"

*****

Kurt runs towards the front gate and is stopped by one of the Scarab knights, "You must stay inside, there is an attack right outside these doors."

Kurt tosses him aside, "That's exactly why I'm headed out there." Kurt barrels through the door to witness a giant werewolf biting off the arms of one of the invisible three. He quickly shoots the werewolf in the eyes followed by him taking several shots at the Vampires taking them down one by one. The twin brothers take turns forming and splitting to attack and defend the Church from the sea of monsters. The now one-armed member of the invisible three takes his bow staff in one arm and drives it straight into the heart of a vampire attacking him from behind.

Kurt is knocked down by a werewolf pouncing on him, "Get off me you mangy mutt!" He growls out. He took a hold of its jaws and pulled them apart staring down the throat of this beast. Mustering up enough strength to snap his jaw open injuring the beast long enough to grab his guns and shoot him right between the eyes. Kurt turns to see the one-armed Scarab knight slashed across his back, then chest, then his head bitten clean off by three werewolves surrounding him. He runs over to attack.

Elizabeth runs into the kitchen and into Baxter, "Where's Maria? This place is being–"

"Attacked, I know and I'm grabbing Maria and we have to go. Where's Kurt?"

Just then they hear a scream, they both run in the direction of the screaming child hoping it isn't Maria. They bust through the kitchen doors to find a slain Sasha, slashed throat and Vexor standing with Fahban who now has Maria in his clutches. Baxter pulls his gun out.

"Mr. Wordsworth, that would be foolish seeing as you could hurt the girl, or worse we could. We're leaving but feel free to let Kurt know I left him a little surprise. Now let's go, Fahban."

Elizabeth screams out reaching for Maria, "You bastard let her go!"

Fahban casts a spell and a doorway appears and they disappear through it, sending out force as Elizabeth and Baxter drop to the floor. Outside the battle rages on as Kurt, the remaining two of the invisible three and the twin Mages try to fend off

the last of the hoard. Other Scarab Knights have come to their aid and the tides of battle turn. Baxter and Liz run outside to inform Kurt of the bad news; Kurt turns to them as they come through the door, but he hears a loud roar. A doorway appears and out steps Stonehenge the giant troll. Kurt pissed off looking up, "Oh shit." He begins to fire shots at Stonehenge, but the bullets just bounce off of its skin.

"Not good!" screams Baxter as he begins shooting at the beast. Stonehenge is now stomping on Scarab Knights and swatting them around left and right (headed towards Kurt and Baxter). They are no match for the trolls' strength and ferocious nature. The twin mage split to attack on both sides of the troll, but they are quickly slammed into the walls by Stonehenge. Liz calls out in anger and begins to shoot the beast in the face making him angry. Stonehenge begins running towards Danger and his friends, knocking everyone in his path down or in the air.

Kurt yells out, "Liz, Baxter get back in the Church!" Before he knows it, Stonehenge comes barreling through tackling Kurt through the doors of the Church. Liz and Baxter run to Kurt's aid only to see him in the clutches of Stonehenge being swung around like a ragdoll. The troll throws him through some tables and then through a pillar. It begins to beat his chest and roar as Liz and Baxter shoot at the troll in the back. Now he turns to them and charges at them. They both move quickly as the beast slams through another pillar and through a wall trying to escape the oncoming bullets. Baxter follows it through. While it is stunned and distracted the Scarab Knights begin attacking it outside, Liz goes over to Kurt to check on him, "Kurt are you alright?"

Kurt grunts and removes a slab of wood and stone off of himself, "Where's Maria?"

Liz now with tears in her eyes, "Vexor took her with some Nightstalker disguised as a Scarab."

Kurt now looks pissed off more than before, Baxter is tossed back into the church. Baxter looks up at Kurt and Liz looking down at him, "Okay this bastard is tough and he's not going down."

Liz looks over at the troll, "His exterior is impenetrable, but his insides might not be."

Kurt nods and grabs his grenade, "If I can get him to slow down and open his mouth then it's tick tick boom." Stonehenge stomps back into the room coming for the trio, just then golden chains of light come out of nowhere wrapping around the Trolls hands, legs bring in him down and restraining him as well as around its throat. Out from the sanctuary tent emerges Magnas with his hands glowing, "Now while he is down take your best shot and end this beast Kurt."

Kurt smiles as he runs up and chucks the grenade in the mouth of Stonehenge, "Hope you like grenades for breakfast you son of a bitch." Kurt turns and runs toward everyone telling them to take cover. Soon after Stonehenge eyes open wide with fear as his body explodes from the inside out body parts fly everywhere. The troll is dead. The injured and beaten down Scarabs all gather in what's left their dining hall, and Magnas speaks with them, "Our Sanctuary has been infiltrated by evil and in our blind hubris couldn't see a traitor in our midst, that mistake has cost lives and led to the kidnapping of a young girl

we were supposed to take care of. If not for Kurt Danger and his friend many more could have lost would have lost their lives today. For this we owe you a great thanks." They all applaud, Kurt gets up and begins walking out followed by Liz and Baxter.

"It's our fault she's with Vexor, so I'm sorry if I don't have the time to celebrate a victory when we weren't victorious in the first place!" Kurt roars. They all head back to the car; the twin Mage comes to say goodbye to their cousin they embrace the twins opening the gate. The Trio walks through the walls and back through the forest to the car. They all agree on one thing, Vexor must be found and Maria saved.

# Chapter Six

# GO NUTS FOR DONUTS

Chuck's is driving down the highway when he witnesses a purple aura open a hole out of thin air. He recognizes that aura from the guys at the diner, he slows down the car and pulls over on the side of the road. Stepping out the purple hole in the middle of the air, is a well-dressed man, in an all-black and red suit sporting this sinister smile. The  man is followed by a man dressed in all black with that familiar purple aura surrounding him and he has a little girl in his hands. That's the girl from the diner incident. The group gets into a black van that is parked on the road. Chuck realizes this is bad, maybe Kurt Danger is dead and now that girl is on trouble. He watches the van pulls off, and Chuck decides to follow them, he will not allow these guys to hurt that little girl.

Kurt and company are driving trying to figure out where Vexor would've taken her. All silent in their thoughts as Kurt is pissed off, Elizabeth is distraught, and Baxter is determined to retrieve the girl.

Baxter finally breaks, "Kurt do we still have friends at the Bureau?"

Kurt thinks hard for a minute. "Just one, Big Roger. We gotta stop and grab some donuts."

Liz looks at both of them confused, "Donuts?"

Two miles down the road Kurt finds a Donut shop. He goes in and buys a Bakers' Dozen. The team drives off toward a new direction.

Elizabeth asks them, "So why the donuts again?" Baxter and Kurt look at each other laughing hysterically,

Baxter chuckles, "The donuts are for Big Roge. He is an I.T. guy at the Bureau and usually you can find him at the front desk moon lighting as a front desk clerk. They usually kick his ass out cause he's annoying. You're going to use the donuts and your sex appeal to get the information we need."

Elizabeth shakes her head, "No one is that gullible."

Kurt and Baxter begin to laugh again hard, this time it's Kurt that answers her, "Believe me Roger is." The car continues to drive on towards the Bureau headquarters. Arriving letting Liz

out, she walks into the doors of the Bureau, wearing a tight-fitting red dress, red high heels, and red lipstick.

"Red is Roger's favorite color on women, so he will immediately be focused on you and putty in your hands." Elizabeth can hear Kurt's words echo in her head as she walks right up to the front desk. Where a short, round, and portly man in a blue blazer, white shirt, and grey pants uniform sits. Roger notices this vixen walk into the building with such vigor. Each step she took sent shivers down his spine. She had full red lips, hips and thighs that were hugged by the dress she wore. She was incredible, looked exotic and single, he noticed no ring in sight on her hands. And Roger was ready for the challenge.

Liz walks up to the desk speaking with an exaggerated Spanish accent "Hello handsome, I had no idea they'd have somebody this cute working at the door."

Roger smiles, "Well it's not my real position here I just cover these shifts from time to time baby, my name is Roger Newman I'm one of the head honchos of the IT department, honey."

Liz thinks, He sounds disgusting each time he calls himself "flirting" with her. Let me just get this over with. Liz puts on a big smile and she knows she has him right where she wants him.

"Well then Roger you're just the guy I'm looking for. I'm in need of some information so maybe a smart, handsome, and strong guy like yourself can help a girl out with? I mean a favor for a favor of course." She winks as she holds up a box of donuts and opens it to reveal the delicious desserts to Roger.

Roger licks his lips, eyes lighting up at the donuts and the woman holding them. "Exactly what did you need help with hun?"

Elizabeth smiles and rubs Roger's arm with the tips of her fingertips, "I need to find someone in your database, you see I'm a reporter from a local news station and the last lead I got was this Bureau would know the latest location of a man named Lucious Vexor."

Roger makes a face as if he knows exactly who she is referring to, "Well that might be in our private archives hun, that won't be easy...."

Elizabeth leans in further, "Aww Roger I'm sure we can work something out, maybe after I land this huge story you and I can talk on the phone or even over dinner sometime." Roger smiles getting lost in Elizabeth's eyes, "Well in that case I'll go up and find out any information I can pull up for you sweetheart. You wait right here, and I'll be right back with that info for you."

Elizabeth smiles. "Thanks cutie pie I'll be waiting." Roger radios for a quick break and then he leaves with the donuts. He returns twenty minutes later with the information regarding Vexor's whereabouts, including info on the layout and where his chambers are located.

Elizabeth smiles hard, then she kisses him on the cheek and slides a fake cell number in his jacket pocket, "Call me sometime sweet stuff."

Roger smiles and replies, "Yessir sure will baby doll."

Elizabeth makes it back to the car which was parked away from the office of the Bureau as to not be spotted. Once in the

car she hands Baxter the USB, he plugs it into his laptop. As information downloads Baxter says, "Good work Liz, you really put the whammy on Big Rog" Baxter and Kurt laugh as the info loads up and Kurt reads through it all. Baxter says, "Looks like Vexor isn't far at all in fact we can reach him by night fall."

Kurt looks over at Elizabeth and proclaims, "Time to get our little lady back." Elizabeth nods, "But first we're going to need weapons, ammo, and some serious backup."

The team drives back towards the Citadel.

# Chapter Seven

# INTO THE BELLY OF THE BEAST

Driving down the road in pursuit of the van Chuck tries to strategize on how he's going to rescue the girl while making sure not to be spotted by the van. This isn't his first car tailing, so he knows what he's doing. The problem is once the car arrives at his destination what then?

Kurt's driving has them close to their way back to the sanctuary to speak with the Scarab Knights, but first they make a stop at an abandoned gas station. Its sign hanging by one chain, its door gated and boarded-up, and several pump stations are missing. Kurt parks and they get out of the car and listen. Kurt and Baxter walk up to the 3rd and 5th Pump Station. Each grab a pump and a cellar hatch opens in the middle of the station revealing an underground facility. They each head down the ramp towards the service elevator. Once the hatch closes, they enter the elevator and press down. The elevator arrives on the lower level in the doors open to reveal the command center like in the diner but smaller. Kurt goes over to the weapons vault and begins stocking up, Baxter grabs ammunition and Liz tries to reach Samson.

Kurt returns with a bag full of weapons to find a distraught Elizabeth, "Something's wrong Sam's not picking up and there's no sign of him on the radar." Kurt drops his bag and runs over to the monitor and starts fingering some keys.

Elizabeth walks up beside him. "What are you doing?"

Kurt frantically toggles with switches, "Trying to get the camera feed to the diner. Sam always answers no matter what. I felt like there was something wrong for a very long time now." Just then the screens light up and the camera feed appears on screen. Elizabeth says, "Oh my God." The screen shows the aftermath of an exhort attack on the diner, it focused on a slain Samson with his neck slashed and lying on the floor lifeless. Kurt, frustrated, tosses a chair into the wall.

"Vexor!" The (guttural) scream can be heard for miles.

Baxter tries to calm him down, Kurt pushes him away. Kurt sheds tears for the first time since his wife's death 10 years ago. Samson was his mentor, friend, and father figure. Now Vexor has killed his parents, his wife, and now his adoptive father and mentor. Kurt numbly walks over to his bags with guns grabbing a revolver that has an engraving, "To Kurt keep shooting until you can't anymore." This silver revolver was

given to him by Samson when he cocks it back and looks at the screen taking in his mentor and friend one last time, face set he looks at the others.

"Let's go kill this bastard." They walk out of the facility and make their way to the Scarab Knights stronghold.

Vexor's van arrives at his castle, he gets out and is greeted by a creature with a hunchback and a greenish yellow face and sharp teeth. The creature stands four feet tall and is wearing a tattered old tuxedo. Vexor sticks out his hand and the creature kisses his hand, Vexor lifts his hand high in the air, "Oh what a glorious day. Fargus tells them all, every Creature, every demon, vagabond, ghoul, and beast. Tell them all that tonight is a night we celebrate. Tonight, we toast the end of Kurt Danger." Fargus the Hunchback creature stumbles as he tries to inform his master, "Lord V-V-V-V-Vexor," he starts to stutter. Vexor stops him, "Spit it out."

Fargus informs him, "Kurt Danger survived the mountain troll and he is on his way here master."

Vexor stops walking as he turns to Fargus and grabs him by the throat, "How do you know this?"

Fargus chokes out, "Tarok has seen it, he says Kurt Danger lives and the captain of The Bureau says your file has been accessed recently." Vexor screams out in rage and he strangles Fargus to his last breath. He drops the lifeless creature on the ground, "Take the girl to her new room and bring Tarok to me."

The Night Stalker grabs Maria and carries the unconscious girl away, "Yes Lord Vexor." Vexor walks into the castle and the door slams behind him. From up on a hill overlooking the vile castle belonging to the line of Charles Luciano, Chuck has heard everything he needs to hear, and he has seen a flaw in their defenses—an entrance near the sewer area. Chuck knows Danger is on his way, but he needs to secure the girl and now he has an actual plan—to sneak into the sewer area and find his way to the girl. Chuck sneaks down looking around and slipping unnoticed into the water, he opens the gate under the castle covering the sewer entrance he walks in preparing himself for just about anything. The sewer area looks like an old catacomb, dark and eerie complete with a stench of dead carcasses, its walls brown and green, rocks layering its ankle-deep water. Chuck walks in further with his gun and flashlight in hand, his steps are silent and deliberate as to not make any alerting noises. Chuck feels something past him, and he knows it's a rodent, a few more steps in and the smell gets worse, now he can smell the feces and urine from what could only be canines of some sort, as well as death all around him. Just then he senses something or someone else there with him. He's staying still so he can figure out what it is and where exactly this thing is. Finally, he just addresses it.

He calls out, "I know you're here; I can hear you; I don't know what you are but know this, I'm no one's easy prey." Hearing faint laughter all around him, something is circling him and moving fast, almost as if it isn't running at all. The laughter continues and Chuck is sure it sounds like a woman's laughter.

The Voice asks Chuck a question, "Are you friend or foe to the demon?"

Chuck looks around trying to see where the Voice came from. Feeling everything around him change as if the air around him has been altered.

Chuck answers, "I'm no friend to demons, but if you're speaking about that guy who just kidnapped a little girl then I'm definitely a foe."

At his response The Voice appears before him, it's a woman she is draped in a wedding gown and her body is transparent, a light blue. She is a ghost of some form that much Chuck knows. She drifts right up to his face and looks Chuck right in the eyes, "He aims to use the girl as a weapon, he wants to lead an army of monsters into the world and destroy all human life. If you oppose him then I will grant you passage to my entrance." Chuck looks at the spirit confused she wants to help, "Who are you? And why are you helping me?"

The spirit hovers around him, and stares into his eyes deeply, "The demon's name is Vexor and he murdered me on the eve of my wedding, that act has cursed me. My spirit is eternally locked to his until he is killed. Until that time, the time when my love finally kills him, I cannot let him harm another innocent, especially this girl. She is integral to the future of the final battle coming."

Chuck stands in disbelief in a matter of 48 hours he's seen magic, vampires, whatever that thing was that just died, and now a ghost all because of one man—Kurt Danger. Chuck laughs, "Lead the way lady and let's hope I can stop them before it's too late."

The spirit glides towards the wall on the far side of the catacombs and the wall opens to reveal a staircase. "Take these stairs. They lead to a dungeon area where the girl will be kept, free her and return this way do not, I say, do not try to face the demon or his minions alone. You are not equipped enough to handle these monsters."

Chuck begins to walk through the doorway when the spirit stops him coming near his ear, "I ask you one favor, my love is coming for him. I can feel him when you see him next tell him you saw me and that he must finish Vexor."

Chuck turns to the spirit, "Who is your love?"

The spirit whispers in his ear, Chuck's smiles, "Figures." With that Chuck goes up the staircase and the wall closes behind him (leaving him in the dark.)

Meanwhile the trio arrives back at the sanctuary and they are met by Nassir and Egil,

"Cousin you've returned."

Liz nods, "We need to speak with everyone."

Nassir opens the wall and escorts them in, "He has been expecting you."

They walk in, everyone that's left gathered in the dining hall, Elizabeth gets on a table to speak to them all, "Listen, you are my family and we have already asked enough of you in the last few days. But now I come to you asking for your hand in taking down the evil bastard who is responsible for the lives

lost here and the kidnapping of a child. I'm asking you to join me and my friends to truly vanquish this evil and do what the Scarab Knights were created for, vanquishing evil." The crowd shouts excitedly.

Just then Magnas emerges and asks, "May I have a word with Kurt Danger?"

Elizabeth looks at Magnas and Kurt begins walking towards the quarters of Magnas. Magnas sits at a table with a large scroll draped over it, Kurt is asked to sit, he declines. Magnas smiles, "Kurt you truly are a remarkable entity, for which you truly know not how much. The battle you ask my Knights to fight is one battle in a series of battles yet to come. I will grant their assistance but only after you are made aware of the bigger purpose at hand."

Kurt interrupts, "What are you getting at? What bigger purpose?"

Magnas reads from the scroll, "The Demon King will rise from the depths to bring forth his horde to take the world of the light. In this time of hellfire and brimstone, the one who will oppose him will walk the line of savior and martyr. He will give his last breath in battle with the man without a future, the woman with ancient skills, and the young lady who will find her place amongst demons and human beings. Together they will restore order."

Kurt stands there stunned and confused. Magnas walks towards him placing his hand on Kurt's shoulder, "The prophecy is about you, Baxter, Elizabeth and the young lady Maria. You must save her, Kurt. Bring her back to the new sanctuary. You must survive this fight; the girl and you are more important to the final battle than you know."

Kurt shakes his hands off his shoulders, Uninterested "I have no idea what the hell you're talking about. I don't give two shits about something some old guy wrote before I was even born. What I do know is I'm going to save the girl, kill Vexor and anything else that stands in my way. So, save your prophecies and your chosen ones for someone who cares about that bullshit. I got a monster to kill."

With that he turns and walks out.

Magnas whispers. "Yes, you do."

Kurt walks out and silences the crowd taking over Elizabeth's speech, "Listen up I'm going to make this very simple we're walking right into the Devil's Mouth. What I'm asking you to do isn't going to be a walk in a park. I'm asking you to risk your lives so you can get payback on the man who single-handedly lead to every one of your friends and family dying and that little girl being kidnapped on my watch. I know it pisses me off your family and friends were killed on my watch and it should piss you off.

"So, you should join us but know if you come with me expect to die and make sure you take a few of those bastards with you!  If you're lucky and don't die you make sure you kill a little bit more. Simply put we might not make it out alive but I damn sure ain't letting that little girl get hurt by that bastard who's with me?!"

The knights scream out a resounding "Us!"

Elizabeth walks up to Kurt, "You give a good speech, what did my uncle want?"

Kurt turns to her, "Nothing. Just about some bullshit that can wait, let's stock up and ride out. We don't have too much time and it'll take us a few hours to reach Vexor's castle."

Magnas comes out from the sanctuary and says, "No it won't I can create a jump that can get you there quicker but only near the castle as Vexor's power is too strong for anything closer."

Kurt smiles, "Perfect you get us there, we will handle the rest." Walking to the armor room, they prepare for the battle of their lives.

# Chapter Eight
# UNINVITED GUESTS

Chuck finds his way slowly up the staircase to a dungeon area equipped with two cells. It's brown and dirty and smaller than he expected. He scans the room and sees two entrances but only one exit, the way he came. He also sees the little girl and she has noticed him as well, "You're that guy from the Diner." She whispers out.

Chuck says, "Yeah that's me and I'm here to get you out." He walks up to the cell and examines the lock, trying to find out how to break it without making too much noise.

Maria looks at him intently, "You have to hurry before that thing gets back."

Chuck, still messing around with the lock, looks up at her and asks, "What thing?" Just as a wave of something terrible hits his nose.

"It's coming back, you have to hide, you can't kill it."

Chuck looks more closely at her and sees she's noticeably frightened, "I'm getting you out of here." He assures her, the stench getting more pungent, it's closer, and its steps are wide and heavy. He hears a growl as the new visitor enters the room from another entrance. It's a huge Werewolf, dark black fur, deep yellow eyes, a large scar upon its chest, its abdomen is ripped with muscles, and it's tall with a menacing look upon its face. The Werewolf licks his lips and growls, "Who are you?" Hs gruffness echoes in the room. Maria backs away from the front of the cell.

Chuck puts his hand on his gun, "The name's Chuck and I'm taking the girl buddy. So, if you like chasing cars and playing fetch I'd stay out of my way or else today is your last day living."

The beast bursts out in laughter then looks Chuck dead in the eye, "The only person dying today is you Chuck." He charges at Chuck and Chuck fires a shot right at his muzzle dropping him in midair. Chuck turns to the cell, and sees Maria is still scared pointing behind him, he turns around to see the beast rising and spitting out the bullet along with his shot off nose that was instantly healing.

"Oh shit."

The Werewolf licks his lips and says, "Nice shot, too bad you wasted it was poorly aimed. Now you won't get another

shot." He moves like swift lighting upon Chuck before he can do anything. His hand (back) swats Chuck into a wall then he grabs him by his collar and throws him into the other cage door. Just as quickly as he lands the beast grabs him by his throat and tells him, "I'm going to have fun watching your bones break." Throwing him into another wall.

Maria begins to scream and cry hysterically, "Let him go! Leave him alone!" The beast laughed as he pounced on a barely able to stand Chuck and begins to pummel him with rapid strikes to the chest. Chuck is spitting up blood and his ribs are cracking under the intense beating he's taking. Maria drops to her knees and starts to shake as she cries uncontrollably, then she looks up and in a different voice tumbling out low (and menacing)

"Get off him." Her deep and echoing voice reaches the Werewolf and his attention is taken back as he turns to see Maria jump up and dropkick the cage door open, flipping off of a wall and tackling the beast off Chuck. Her demon rage has awakened and now she is ten times stronger than this werewolf, pummeling his face with her bare fists, with each punch they get stronger, heavier, and faster. Chuck begins to stir and begins to pick himself up but looks in shock and awe as he witnesses this young child destroying this large beast. Her punches rain down upon this beast's face, as blood splatters everywhere she smashes this werewolf's skull killing him with her fists.

He walks towards the girl, and her attention is now directed his way, "Leave me alone." Her eyes a glowing red and fangs protruding from her mouth. Just then a large blast of energy hits Chuck in the back and he falls to his knees. Fahban enters and sees Maria who he also hits with a blast that knocks her into a wall knocking her out. He then creates a portal and throws Chuck through it teleporting him into the next cell.

"We will deal with you later, for now I have to take the girl to Vexor." Another portal is created, and he grabs Maria and walks through.

Kurt, Baxter, Elizabeth and the rest of the Scarab Knights that accompanied them emerge from a transportation portal created by Magnas in the woods just outside the castle. Kurt gets in position to scout out their plan. From their position, he can see there are vampire guards watching the tops of the castle, and three werewolves in their full form guarding the castle gate.

There is an area where a waterway access to a sewer area and it seems tampered with which is interesting, he also sees that the sides of the castle are vulnerable if they launch an attack from the sides, but he knows the castle has several guards who would run to protect the entrance and sides once a loud enough distraction is made. Looking back at the sewer, that is where him and Baxter will enter once the chaos ensues.

Turning back to the army he conveys his intel to the entire group reminding them, "If you guys can hold your own for long enough me and Baxter can make our way in and Liz can make it into the back area with twin mages. Once we are in you will fall back to this point and defend the vehicles. We will handle the rest." Turning to Liz and Baxter once everyone agrees and gets in position, "Looks like it's time to crash the party. Let's make some noise."

Fahban teleported them outside of Vexor's quarters, he looks at Vexor's head guard Durbahn, a giant man wearing a large fur coat guarding his door, "Alert Lord Vexor we have an intruder and I need to speak with him." Durbahn growls, taps the intercom on the door, in a raspy growl like voice, "The Nightstalker wishes to see you and to let you know that there is an intruder in the castle. Shall I let him in?"

Vexor's voice crackles through, "Let him in." When Durbahn turns to Fahban he's already made a portal and is going through it, Damien growls angrily.

Fahban stands in the middle of the room.

"We have an issue." Placing the unconscious girl at Vexor's feet.

Vexor looks down at the girl, "Why is she out of her cell? Was the intruder one of Kurt's friends?"

Fahban looks at the unconscious girl.

"This little girl was bludgeoning the werewolf assigned to watch her cell and I had to knock her out. As far as the intruder, I've never seen him before. Looks like he was armed but alone. I knocked him out and placed him in the other cell."

Vexor is intrigued more about the fallen werewolf.

"Is the werewolf dead?" Fahban nods. "Astounding, she's more powerful than I could imagine. Once the procedure is complete, she'll be under my complete control and no longer will her humanity interfere with her true power. With her blood I can create thousands of loyal and totally under my control

warriors." Vexor begins to maniacally laugh at what his plan will do and walks over to the intercom signaling to the lab, "Doctor prepare the lab Fahban is bringing the girl to you and we will begin the procedure."

A voice answers, "Yes, Lord Vexor."

Vexor smiles, his plan finally coming together, but quickly fades as he picks up something in the distance, a whistling noise of something moving in quick.

"Do you hear that?" Just then a rocket explodes into one of the walls of the castle causing the room to shake.

"A rocket?" says Fahban then he hears a familiar horn blown, "Scarab Knights have arrived and where there's rockets there's..."

Vexor gets to his feet, "Kurt Danger.... get the girl to the lab now!"

Durbahn barrels into the room to warn him but Vexor orders him, "Get your pack to the front gates now!" Fahban opens a portal and steps through it with the girl, while Durbahn storms out the room howling to his pack. Vexor whips himself off.


Kurt Danger places the rocket launcher down, Baxter says, "Really a rocket launcher?"

Kurt looks over and shrugs then asks Elizabeth if she's ready, "Yeah we're in position."

Kurt and Baxter make their way down off top of the large cliff and head towards the moat on the side of the fortress.

The Scarab Knights storm the fortress just as the vampires guarding the gate are caught off guard. Bodies clash as the small group of gate protectors of the gate are struck down by the group of Knights. But things are not in their favor for too long, as more Vampires and Werewolves come storming out of the gate.

The Scarab Knights battle with unwavering pride as the beasts bring in their own fury. A Werewolf with dark grey hair and a huge build jumps up and pounces on a Scarab knight biting his face off. Another Scarab Knight drives his sword in the heart of a Vampire killing the beast and without any hesitation he plunges his sword into another. A bow and arrow wielding knight fires her arrows with precision into the brains of 3 werewolves and she continues to fire upon the surrounding vampires killing them as well. A swarm of vampires overwhelm two knights grabbing them and slashing one neck and snapping the other.

The werewolves are harder to take down as they move with a more beastly speed circling the knights. One of the knights known as Richochus counters out a spell creating a glowing hole in mid- air from out of this hole comes golden tentacles with spikes and scales upon them. Which grab many of the evil beasts and suck them into the void with it. Another knight named Karvas whispers a spell that summons golden lightning from the sky blasting some of the monsters back. The one with the arrow is named Dulcet shifts her hands so they look like a shadow puppet and her bow is illuminated and she begins shooting golden arrows of pure light. The one with the swords begins spinning them and generating bright lightning and he goes on to slash down a couple more beasts. They look as if they've won until they hear a very familiar roar, another mountain troll? They look and burst through the gates, is not one troll, it's two mountain trolls bigger than the one they faced in the battle for the sanctuary.

Meanwhile Liz and her cousins the twin mages are now cutting a hole into the side wall with magic. They all hear the trolls.

"Go Liz I will return to the front to assist go save Kurt." says the Twin Mages. Liz nods and hugs her family once more, then she rushes into the fortress to help. The Twin Mages return to the battle at the gate. Kurt and Baxter are sticking to their plan on the other side and have made their way to the grate covering the sewer entrance.

Baxter notices the grate has been pulled back wide enough for someone to fit through, he says "Looks like our entrance was already made for us." Kurt nods and they make their way in. They begin to step into this dark sewer area. Kurt and Baxter turn on their mini flashlights and prepare their guns. Walking lightly as to not make much noise, Kurt's eyes and nose are working double time to be aware of their unknown surroundings. Baxter steps in something that squishes beneath his feet, "Ugh I'm so over this already, it reeks of shit, piss and..."

Kurt interrupts, "Death, a lot of death."

The spirit that spoke to Chuck wanders the area where the little girl was held captive, she sees the carnage and Chuck in the other cell. She attempts to wake him, but he is unconscious, just then she senses a small pack of Werewolves heading towards

the sewer entrance. She knows their plan is to attack the armies from behind but it's not the army she is now worried about, it is her love. She felt his presence and knows he is here now in the sewer and she must warn him.

Kurt and Baxter continue on through this sewer area, Baxter is too focused on the surroundings to notice Kurt has suddenly come to a complete halt in front of him that he bumps into Kurt, "Hey man why'd you stop?" says Baxter. Kurt feels weird, he smells a scent he shouldn't, he feels a presence he shouldn't, but he does. Kurt opens his eyes wide and begins to turn side to side flashing the light around, Baxter taps him concerned, "Kurt what is going on man let me know what we are dealing with."

Just then the spirit appears before Kurt's eyes, "Hello Kurt."

Kurt is shocked he hasn't seen her face in years, "Is it really you? Sarah?"

The glowing spirit puts her hand on his face, "Yeah it's me Killer, you look tired Kurt." Looking him over. Kurt smiles, "You look as beautiful as the day I first laid eyes on you, ladybug."

Baxter looks at this from behind and asks Kurt again, "Kurt what's going on man?"

Sarah knows time is of the essence, "Hey Killer we don't have too much time, listen the one you call Chuck attempted to rescue the little girl but was subdued. The girl is now in the laboratory and Vexor is going to transfer the demonic powers from her to himself, killing the girl in the process. You need to rescue the little girl soon. I can lead you to the Laboratory but there is a small pack of Werewolves heading towards this way you guys have to get past them first."

Kurt nods bracing himself, "Baxter look we got company coming in the form of a small pack of furballs. Let's get rid of them then Sarah is going to lead us to the girl."

Baxter still looks confused, "Okay wait so your dead fiancée is talking to you and is now going to lead us to the girl… oh yeah you have lost your mind buddy."

Kurt ignores him, "Here they come." Bounding around a corner comes six werewolves, teeth bearing in full beast form on all fours. Kurt begins firing and so does Baxter. Their bullets strike their targets in their bodies but not the heads due to the way they're charging and grouped together they can't seem to get clear enough shots. Kurt notices this as they keep coming, "Damn it! We need space, Baxter I'm going to clear a path, grab your shades on three."

Kurt grabs a spherical object that is orange and purple, it glows and when he presses it the glow illuminates more as it starts to whirl, "3!" Him and Baxter grab their shades as he throws the object at the ceiling in front of the group of beasts. The object explodes upon impact and blinding orange light lights up the whole sewer. It blinds the beasts and they fall one by one. The object was a sun burst bomb harnessing an ultraviolet and military grade flashbang power. It blinds the beasts as well as disorientates and causes sickness to the affected party. Writhing on the ground, Kurt and Baxter walk up to the beasts and execute them with shots to the brains.

Baxter turns to Kurt and says, "Now let's get to the girl. Is your dead fiancée ready to lead us?" Still skeptical but rolling with it.

She whispers in Baxter's ear, "As a matter a fact I am Baxter. This way, follow me guys." Baxter jumps back, turning around to face the voice, and now he can see what Kurt sees, "Okay yep I've lost it too." He shakes his head, "Let's do this no turning back now." Kurt laughed and they began to follow her to the secret passage.

# Chapter Nine
# MONSTER MASH

The battle outside rages on as the monsters begin taking the advantage against the Scarab Knights with the addition of the two mountain trolls. One of the humongous trolls grabs two knights and smashes them together crushing their bodies and splattering them in his hands. This horrific sight frightens other knights as they see their friends mutilated before them.

The other troll swats away a few more knights as others are taken down by werewolves or vampires. Suddenly bounding around the corner comes the twin mage. He instantly splits in two and casts spells conjuring up golden glowing giants who each go head to head with the large beasts. Each construct begins by pushing the trolls and then punching the trolls with a mighty strike knocking them back. This newfound tide is inspiring courage that helps them start to charge back towards the swarm of monsters. Richochus and Karvas create glowing swarms of Scarab constructs that begin to attack their multiple enemies at once. Dulcet continues to fire her golden arrows and the werewolves and vampires begin to fall one by one.

Inside of the castle, Elizabeth is walking through the corridors down these elaborate hallways adorned with red and gold accents. There are several pictures of Vexor's ancestral lineage. There are several statues and the stench of this place is putrid and reminiscent of dried blood and death. Elizabeth feels sick to her stomach but more determined than ever to save Maria. She begins to walk fast looking for something, anything, that resembles a doorway to the rooms below the castle where she believes Maria would be held captive.

Just then a swirling purple circle appears out of nowhere, out steps Fahban. Elizabeth stops, and casts a spell around her hands, they glow in a golden hue as she casts an energy bow and arrow and fires it at him. Another purple energy suddenly comes forth from his body and grabs the arrow of light sent by her. Fahban turns his head to her and smiles statistically, "Lizzy it's nice to see you too." Elizabeth quickly casts another spell this time conjuring energy daggers she begins to throw with precision at Fahban, but he too creates a spell quickly and begins to block her daggers with his purple energy hand constructs. Fahban laughs, "You're quite the angry one but the question is are you angry because I betrayed you or are you angry because your people fell for my betrayal?"

Elizabeth screams out in rage, "You murderer!" A golden blade conjures in her right hand as she charges him. He laughs sarcastically as he creates a portal quickly and teleports himself

out of her way. His laughter fills the halls, "You'll have to do better than that little lady if you want to exact your revenge. He appears above her and blasts her with a ball of his purple energy. She falls to the ground.

"You will die by my hands Fahban." Fahban smirks at her, walking towards her purple energy flowing from his hands. His mistake, Elizabeth can now feel his energy and she now knows exactly how to track him.

He shoots another blast at her but this time she dodges the blast and throws her glowing daggers at him, which he continues to block but this time she keeps the barrage coming with one hand while the other conjures another blade. Steadily blocking the daggers and laughing at her he mocks her.

"Is that all they taught you in Scarab Knight School? Pathetic." Just then Liz charges at him with a thrust of the blade which he quickly uses another portal to nearly escape. Liz smiles, when the other portal opens Fahban has conjured a blade of his own to strike her from behind, but he underestimated his adversary. As he exits the portal ready to thrust his blade in her back she turns instantly and rolls into a forward thrust of her own energy blade straight into his heart.

"To answer your question, no they taught me how to trace energy and this nifty little move I just used to kill you. You bastard." Fahban falls out of the portal and lands on the ground lifeless. Elizabeth walks away from his lifeless body and continues on her towards Maria. Outside the battle rages on as the remaining Scarab Knights look to have the upper hand in the battle with the monstrous horde raining down on them. The two mountain trolls slowly make their way back to their feet as the constructs created by the twin mage begin to charge at them. Now the trolls smash into the ground causing the earth to shake violently which causes everyone to lose their balance. This balance shift causes the control over the constructs to wane, the trolls charge at the twins and one swats Eigel into a wall. His construct evaporates as he is knocked unconscious. His brother Nassir turns his attention to the other mountain troll and casts a spell of blinding light into its eyes and gets his construct to grab the other by the arms and pin it against the ground, "Richochus, now!!!"

Richochus sees the beast down and he conjures up a giant sword and stabs the beast in its eyes wounding it now the beast is enraged and he charges up violently breaking the grip of Nassir's construct and turning towards Nassir grabbing a chunk of the earth and hurtling towards Nassir who only has seconds to move before he is crushed. His construct is then grabbed by both blinded trolls and torn apart. Then the trolls stomp on Richochus who turns to check on Nassir. Karvas is taken down by a werewolf who catches him off guard by the death of his friend and he is smashed on his back then his stomach by another werewolf then lastly grabbed by another wolf and his head is bitten off. Nassir sees the shift of the battle and begins to conjure a spell that opens a portal he yells, "Knights fall back fall back!!!!!" Those that can escape while their friends are slaughtered by the beasts and monsters surrounding them fall into the portal. Nassir grabs his brother and he is the last through the portal as it closes whispering back, "Liz it's up to you and Kurt now."

Kurt, Baxter, and Sarah's spirit arrive in the same room where Maria was originally held. When they arrive, Kurt sees the bludgeoned body of a dead werewolf and he says, "Whatever killed him beat him with their bare hands."

A voice from the cage interrupts the group, "The little girl that you're here to save did that to that thing I saw it with my own eyes. I see you finally made it to the party and you brought your two buddies. Hey Kurt, it is Kurt, right?"

Kurt looks and sees one of the guys sent to bring him in from the diner a few days ago, "Yeah it's Kurt, you look like you've seen better days. I don't think I caught your name last time you were after me."

Chuck looks at him with an intensity, "It's Chuck."

Kurt stares back at him with the same intensity, "Well Chuck you mind telling me what you're doing here?"

Chuck stands up slowly, "Well I was looking for you when I happened upon some creep using the same magic that those fools that killed my partner did in the diner. I saw him and some other dressed up creep carrying the kid from the diner. I knew something was wrong, so I followed them back here. I snuck in and met her," gesturing to Sarah, "in the sewers." He looks right at Sarah's spirit; Kurt turns back to her then back to him.

"You can see her?"

Chuck nods yes and continues, "She's the one that told me to try to save the kid and that's when I ran into that dead mutt on the ground. I almost had the girl to safety when that thing attacked me and nearly killed me when the girl jumped on him and wrecked him like I've never seen before but before I could do anything that punk with that magic knocked me into this cell and took the girl."

Kurt looks at the lifeless body of the werewolf. He turns to Chuck, he aims his gun at the lock blasting off the lock, "I'm sorry about your partner, but right now we need to save that little girl from these monsters. If you're still salty with me afterwards you can try to take me in, but I need your help okay?"

Chuck smiles as he walks out of the cell, "Fine by me all I care about now is killing one of those beasts and once the girl is safe, I got bigger fish to fry."

Kurt passes him an extra firearm, "Next time you see one aim right between the eyes, and you'll get your fill." The newly formed trio walk through a corridor that leads them to the lower levels where the lab lies. Vexor walks into the laboratory with tons of jars with green, red, and blue liquids from the covering creatures and experiments from Doctor Hyde. Hyde is a tall slender man with brown hair and a handsome face with the exception of a small scar on his right side of his face. He is the head scientist for Vexor and all of his extreme experiments. Vexor sees Maria knocked out and strapped down to a medical bed with wires hooked up to the straps and back to machines with weird liquid tubes on top and thousands of buttons and knobs. Vexor smiles removing his robe and rolling up his sleeves and laying down on the other table next to Maria,

"Let's not waste another minute Hyde. I have an unexpected guest and I want to try out my new powers on the bastard."

Hyde nods as he straps Vexor down and sticks needles into his arm and begins to turn knobs on the left side of the machine, "Commencing the transfer."

Hyde goes over to Maria and places nods on her temples and presses buttons on the right side of the machine. The machine begins to whirl loudly, it lights up and the red and green fluid on top begins to bubble and shake. The machine sends electrical power throughout each side as it shakes and gets louder. Just then a red electrical pulse shoots through the machine and through Maria shocking the young girl without mercy. Maria shrieks in pain as her eyes widen open and pain shoots through her body.

Elizabeth walks into a hallway with three Vampires who she quickly dispatches with a jump off of the left wall and a stab with her energy daggers, one down leads to another being pinned against a wall by a thrown energy dagger and the other she charges and flips over her stabbing her in the process. After the Vampires fall, she hears the screams of Maria, she runs following the scream but wonders if she's too late.

Kurt and the others arrive at a wall covered in ancient hieroglyphs, Sarah's spirit floats over to the wall and turns to Kurt, "Once I open this wall, I cannot go with you any further his powers would sense me and regain his hold on me. Through this corridor will lead you right into the laboratory. He has begun the transfer and you must stop him Kurt." They watch as she touches the wall and the hieroglyphs begin to light up and disappear followed by the stones on the wall folding into one another creating a doorway. Kurt walks up to Sarah smiling, "I will finish him hun, and save the girl. Thank you gorgeous, let's hope we see each other again." He walks through the doorway with Baxter following behind smiling at Sarah. Chuck walks towards the doorway and stops, he turns to Sarah's spirit and asks, "Does he know?"

Sarah's spirit says, "No. It's your choice on whether he should know or not." With that Chuck turns back and walks through the doorway.

Elizabeth ends up outside a corridor where she smells several werewolves. She carefully walks up to the side of the wall and begins to do a spell to mask her scent from the beasts. She peeks around the corner and sees five werewolves standing guard in full beast form in front of a giant door. She hears the screams of Maria again; she must get inside there but five might be too much for her alone. She has to get inside, but how?

Kurt, Baxter, and Chuck walk through a cave-like tunnel entrance and they can hear the screams of the girl. Kurt begins to run knowing this is it. They end up at a door that is locked, "Damn." Kurt says as he grabs a grenade, "Well so much for the element of surprise." Baxter chuckles. Kurt warns, "Stand back."

They all retreat back as he throws the grenade from a safe distance. BOOM! The door blows wide open splinters and debris fly everywhere. Inside the demon energy is being transferred from Maria into Vexor and his body surges with power, as the girl's screams get weaker. Tarok squeals in delight, "The transfer is nearly complete Master."

Just then a large wooden door that was previously locked, blasts open with debris flying everywhere and sending Hyde and Tarok flying and ducking the explosion. A piece of debris

smashing into the console of the machine causing it to spark and explode shutting it down. Out from the chaos and smoke emerges Kurt Danger and his two accompanying gun wielding partners.

While Elizabeth is still trying to figure out a way to get past these werewolf guards a huge explosion happens from inside. The werewolves are stunned, and they quickly open the doors and charge in to protect their master. Liz knows what this means, Kurt and Baxter have made it. She hurries through the door ready for a fight. When she gets through the door, she scans the room, the laboratory is in a state of disarray, there is a huge hole where a door once stood. Standing there instead are her friends Kurt and Baxter alongside that guy who was previously hunting them, on the floor lies a small ugly creature in a brown tattered robe with a weird looking man in a lab coat. There is a machine that looks badly damaged that seemed to be hooked up to both Vexor and Maria who lied there unconscious. Tarok stands and sees Kurt Danger and crew with guns drawn, he turns and sees the Werewolves and yells at them, "Protect your master!"

The werewolves howl and begin charging at the trio. Kurt turns towards Baxter and Chuck, "Baxter, Chuck handle then I'm going after the kid." Baxter begins shooting at the beasts, Chuck scans the room and notices the width of the room. The werewolves split up and begin running in a pattern dodging Baxter's gunfire. Chuck sees what they are doing, "They're going to surround us."

Kurt is blocked by one of the beasts and Kurt shoots at it immediately, but the beasts are agile and very fast. Dodging his bullets and swats at Kurt's' guns out of his hands and then slaps him into a wall. Two of the other werewolves run around Baxter and are now in front and behind him almost stalking him. Baxter thinks for a moment and knows he's carrying something that can help with the current situation, but he might not have enough time. Chuck now has two werewolves walking towards him, he sees the sparkling and flaming machine behind them and knows he can use that, but he must get behind them first. Just then Liz takes aim with an energy arrow that one of the beasts didn't see as it goes right through his ear and brain killing it instantly, the other werewolf standing next to it turns towards the direction of Elizabeth and Chuck charges him tackling him into the broken machine the beast is thrown into the electrified, burning machine instantly setting it on fire. It begins to howl out in pain screaming and whimpering out loud till the machine explodes again blowing a huge hole in the werewolf's back and knocking him unconscious.

The other werewolves distracted by all of this lets Baxter pull out his flash bang grenade and he tosses it at the werewolf in front of him. It explodes upon contact with the beast blinding him and Baxter takes advantage of this and shoots it in the kneecaps and then right between the eyes killing him. The one behind him charges him and Elizabeth throws a few energy daggers at the beast giving Baxter the opportunity to shoot him right between the eyes. The werewolf that was fighting Kurt charges Elizabeth ferociously, but Chuck begins shooting it with Baxter joining in. The beast is annoyed by the gunfire and roars as he is shot in the chest. Kurt gets up and he yells taunting him, "Hey Furball how about round two?" The werewolf turns back to Kurt and looks at him with a fierce intensity.

Kurt yells into the room, "Stop firing, he's mine." They all stop, and the beast laughs as he charges at Kurt, Kurt stares at him and grabs on the hilt of a dagger Kurt is tired of this and as the beast draws nearer, he prepares to take it out with malice. The beast goes in for the pounce and as he comes down upon Kurt, his team gasps but Kurt has already driven the dagger through the beast's skull right between its eyes killing it instantly. He throws the dead carcass off of himself, gets up and grabs his pistols to continue but before he can turn, he hears a familiar clap and laughter.

The clapping and maniacal laughter is coming from a now awake Vexor who now has glowing red eyes and his aura begins to surround the room. The laughter gets more hysterical as Vexor seemingly floats out of his bed and lands. Still clapping he speaks, "You are freaking amazing Kurt, like truly I wish you and I worked together because you are the baddest of the bad asses. A murderous unforgiving bastard of destruction that truly lives up to his namesake you are truly a Monster hunter. Congratulations for all of this so far but alas it was futile. The girl's powers are mine and she is dead, and NOW SO ARE YOU!"

# Chapter Ten

# VEXOR: THE TRUE PRINCE OF ALL VAMPIRES

The red aura that surrounded Vexor has the same power of whenever Maria transformed. Kurt and Baxter immediately begin firing at Vexor, but this isn't regular Vexor anymore. His power and speed have increased tremendously, he dodges their bullets as if they were shooting in slow motion. Vexor laughs maniacally as he begins to glide across the room with lightning speed.

Elizabeth stares in disbelief, "He's moving so fast I can hardly see him at all."

Kurt, beyond furious, continues to shoot at him. "Stand still you bastard!"

Vexor laughs and in the blink of an eye he moves in with a forceful gut punch to Kurt making him spit out blood and drop his weapons in pain. Vexor next moves with such speed upon Baxter within seconds, Baxter has no time to block the roundhouse kick to the face which sends him bouncing across the floor into the wall. Chuck fires a shot that makes it very close but Vexor still dodges it instantly. Vexor smiles over at Chuck, "I don't think we've met, allow me to introduce myself. I'm Vexor Prince of all Vampires and soon to be king." Flashing right next to Chuck smacking him into a wall.

Elizabeth looks over at Maria, then looks around the room where Kurt, Baxter, and Chuck are all laying there, and it leaves her stunned. Vexor notices and walks over, slowly, taking his sweet time, "This power is just the tip of the iceberg, and I'm going to savor this moment for what it is." (Circling her as she tries to process the turn of events) "The killing of Kurt Danger followed by the final destruction of your miserable clan and finally being recognized as the king of all Vampires."

Elizabeth drops to her knees and the tears start to flow from her eyes, "No need for tears, I'll make sure your death is quicker than Kurt's death, you can take comfort in that. Just know the little bitch didn't die in vain."

Elizabeth then begins to shake, her fist clench, her teeth grit. A faint glow starts to surround her, her inner aura building. Her tears dry as she stands. "You are evil personified and as a Scarab Knight I was born to eradicate evil like you. Killing the

girl was your first mistake, disrespecting her was your last." A blinding light wraps around her body, Vexor shields his eyes for a second only to uncover them and see a bright glowing gold hue aura around Elizabeth's body. She begins to speak ancient spells as her hands glow and she releases her fist to spread the room with golden arrows firing from her hands, thousands of them as they fire towards Vexor who can barely dodges and is struck by a few.

He drops to one knee on the impact, "Fuck this."

He charges at her dodging the other arrows and punching her with the same immense force but instead of her falling or being launched she turns her head towards him looking un-phased. She conjures up a golden chain wrapping it around Vexor's throat throwing him into a wall. Elizabeth creates two swords of energy and charges at Vexor, but he is back on his feet quickly and he kicks her right in the face followed by another punch, then as her body is turned around by the punch, he drives his knee into her back. Before she can get her bearings Vexor appears at her side, punt kicking her in the ribs sending her body flying, her glowing around her disappears.

Kurt stirs and as he sees Liz laying there barely able to move, he grabs his dagger and charges Vexor from behind but Vexor blocks him before he can reach instantly appearing on his left side attacking with a barrage of fists. He grabs Kurt's' throat and lifts him high in the air, "You and your friends have annoyed me for far too long." Squeezing Kurt's throat cutting off his air, Elizabeth conjures up energy blasts and blasts him into a wall making him release his grip on Kurt dropping him to the floor. On the other side Baxter begins to stir and notices the damage around him then the fight in front of him.

Elizabeth continues to fire balls of Scarab energy at Vexor and each ball explodes upon contact. She's hitting him with all of her energy and strength she has, all of her anger and rage as she continues to fling those powerful energy balls at Vexor. The wall behind Vexor crumbles and Vexor falls back in the rubble. Elizabeth drops to one knee exhausted and hoping that did enough damage to him so they can grab Maria and go. But she begins to hear his sinister laugh coming from the rubble.

Vexor laughs coming out of the rubble his shirt completely destroyed and glowing with demon energy, "Now that was pretty amusing. No, really you definitely are good missy in another life you and me would've been quite the dynamic duo. But alas this has gone on way too long; I have a world to conquer and you're standing in the way of my greatest revenge. Danger dies today and you can't stop that because you die NOW!"

He rushes her and before she can conjure anything, she is struck with a left-handed chop across her face that knocks her back into a wall. He follows it up with a flurry of attacks with his fist to her torso pinning her. Every punch carves a crater of her body into the stone wall larger and every blow comes faster and stronger than the last. His punches make her spit up blood from the internal injuries he's inflicting and her ribs crack under this beating finally having her fall unconscious.

Baxter watches in pure torment, enraged, he gets up and grabs his gun, firing shots at Vexor but Vexor dodges with blinding speed. Vexor rushes him kicking him deep in the chest

grabbing him by his afro and slams his face into a wall then into the floor below. Vexor laughs hysterically, as he lifts up Baxter who is bleeding all over from his busted open face to his insides. He flings him into another wall like discarded garbage. (He lies still.) Vexor turns to Tarok and tells him, "Prepare my celebration ceremony robes. Tell the horde of monsters outside to make their way back in the party is about to commence." Tarok smiles and rushes out to do as his Master says. Vexor walks over to Kurt and he bends down, "Kurt Danger, legendary monster hunter, lying here bloody, battered, and beaten by the Vampire who killed his fiancé. Pathetic."

Kurt grabs his dagger as Vexor picks him up by his hair to look Kurt in the eyes, "Now it's time to finally end this. Goodbye, you worthless piece of shit." Kurt now close enough to strike, let Vexor lift him and then without hesitation he drives his dagger into Vexor's neck. Vexor drops him and roars in pain. He yanks the dagger out as the blood pours from his wound he turns angrily to Kurt, "You bastard, how could I be that stupid. That was your last gasp? Well now I'm going to make you suffer." Kurt grabs his pistol and tries to shoot him but Vexor grabs his arm and breaks it over his shoulder. Kurt yells out in pain, grabbing his face and knees him right in the face. Kurt stumbles back now his vision is blurry from the blood pouring out trying to get his balance again (for another strike) but Vexor rushes him grabs his good arm and swings him into the wall and launches with a gut punch.

Flashing over and grabbing Kurt by the throat lifting him up and choke slamming him into the ground. He begins to stomp

on his back repeatedly, "You old decrepit Bastard, I am going to remove you from my existence."

Vexor picks him up with one hand holding him against the wall, "I have thought about this repeatedly everyday hoping for the day I could hear your bones crumble at my own hands. "Landing another punch, he looks at Kurt (questioning), "Do you have anything else left to say before I finish you off?"

Kurt manages to smile through his bloody mouth and battered face, he spits blood right in Vexor's face, "You talk too much you fang-faced Bitch." This makes Vexor laugh hysterically almost to the point of madness. Flinging Kurt over his shoulder onto the hard floor below. Vexor mounts Kurt and begins pummeling Kurt. However, each blow became weaker than the last unbeknownst to Vexor. Elizabeth wakes and can only watch from across the room. Baxter turns his body and realizes his friend is getting beaten to death and he can do nothing to stop it. Chuck wakes up barely able to move from his beat down.

Is all lost? Did they fail?

From behind Vexor, a small voice fills the room.

"Get off of him."

Vexor stops mid-punch turning his head towards the medical beds where he was once strapped in besides Maria. What he saw shocked him, it was impossible, he thought to himself.

"You!"

Elizabeth looked at the sight of Maria in disbelief whispering out her name noticing she had an orange glow surrounding her. Vexor smirks, "Looks like you still have some of that wonderful energy to give me. Perfect. I'll make sure to get the last bit you have before killing you but first let me get back to killing Kurt."

He turns back and Maria screams out her voice stronger, "GET OFF OF HIM NOW!" A surge of power explodes from her body and knocks Vexor off of Kurt into a wall. Maria begins to levitate off of the bed all the wires flying off of her body. She floats till she lands besides Kurt; she touches his face and Kurt looks through one eye, "Hey Kiddo sorry I got here so late but I'm here and I'll finish him off okay?"

Maria with tears in her eyes, "No need to be sorry. It's okay I will finish this; you just rest big guy." She then looks up at Vexor as he begins to stand, her stare at him fierce and vengeful. Before he can fully stand, Maria moves on him with the same speed he has and now she has him by the throat.

Vexor looked at Maria with disbelief, struggling to talk, choked out, "How is this possible? You shouldn't have this power." Maria squeezes his throat tighter and tosses him into another wall.

Maria is upon him quickly punching him in the face repeatedly, "You're evil. You will pay for what you did to my friends." She then grabs him by his hair and punches him directly to the face smashing his head into the wall. Maria turns to see Baxter and Elizabeth getting up and she hurries to each of their sides.

Coming up to Baxter, "Are you okay?" Baxter laughs but realizes it hurts to breathe. He grabs his rib area, "I'm fine shorty, go check on Liz." She nods and runs to Liz. "Liz!" Elizabeth looks at her and smiles with tears in her eyes then hugs her tightly, "You gave me quite the scare missy. Listen up, go get Kurt and the guy over there and let's get out of here before…"

Vexor rushes Maria before anyone can even see it coming. Vexor hits her into a wall and digs his knee deep into Maria's chest. Grabbing her and flying her through the ceiling she hits the wood ceiling forcing her to fall to the floor with heavy force and speed. She hits the ground with a thud making Liz and Baxter scream out "Maria!!!"

Vexor comes down with a strong stomp onto the child. Vexor is delighted at his triumph and his inevitable victory over his greatest foe. He begins to walk towards Kurt again laughing, "That was close. I almost thought that little bitch had me beat. Now back to the business of killing you."

As he reaches Kurt, Maria's eyes open and she flips back up, "And I thought I told you not to touch him."

Vexor turns shocked and his smile fades at the sight of her getting up, "Oh you're an annoying little problem, aren't you?" He rushes her seemingly moving as fast as before but that's only to the eyes of Baxter and Liz that notices he's slowed down. Maria rushes him as well and they collide. Outside Tarok arrives with a portal as he instructs the horde of monsters to follow him to the master for his celebration.

On the hill that the knights retreated to Nassir sees this unfolding and thinks the worst. He conjures a silent spell as

a golden Scarab appears and follows Tarok and the monster horde through the transportation portal. As Vexor and Maria get up from knocking each other down Charles stirs and gets up to see this battle taking place and he scans the room to see a beat up and battered Baxter and Elizabeth as well as a badly wounded and injured Kurt Danger. He walks slowly over to his gun on the floor, then he walks over to Baxter who is nearest to him.

Maria looks at Vexor and knows this has to end because her newfound power seems to be dwindling. She prepares herself for his attack ready to finish this. Vexor stares at her breathing heavily, speaking to himself, "How is it she's this powerful? I took most of the demon energy from her and it's like she's even more powerful than before. I have to kill her quickly. This cannot go on forever that's for sure. Time to end this."

He leans down and runs straight at her full speed. Baxter looks perplexed at this sight, "So the girl's not dead and she's still got a lot of fight in her I see." says Chuck from the right.

Baxter turns to him, "Yeah. How you holding up?"

Chuck laughs, "I'm feeling like a mac truck hit me. But I look better than you and Kurt." Baxter smirks and scans the room spotting his friend on the ground. Baxter walks over slowly to Kurt, "Hey Chuck can you check on Elizabeth over there? I'll check on Kurt." Chuck nods walking over to Liz.

Maria and Vexor fight as she dodges the wall before Vexor goes to strike her again. Vexor chases her down, just missing striking her as she is slightly faster than him. Finally, he is able to tackle her to the floor, but this leads to him being close enough for Maria to knee him in his testicles, "No matter what power you may have Vexor, you're still a male." Vexor groans in pain as Maria kicks him in the face and launches him into the broken machinery and lab equipment used to transfer her power.

Chuck gets to Elizabeth and he helps her stand up fully taking care of her injuries. He notices her eyes have not strayed from Maria, "She seems to be handling herself just fine, but we need to get out of here soon don't you think?"

Elizabeth snaps out of it and turns to him, "You're right... I think if Vexor gets worried enough, he will soon call for reinforcements and in the condition we are in, we just can't withstand another huge battle."

Baxter makes his way to Kurt Danger and starts to shake him, "Wake up old man we need to get the girl and go."

Danger begins to stir and groans in pain, "Vexor has to die Baxter, I'm not leaving till he's dead"

"Well Buddy you ain't been doing so well with him since his power up and you might get your wish if Maria has anything to say about it." Kurt makes his way up on his feet assisted by Baxter. He sees Maria grab Vexor from the machine rubble and throw him across the room with ease. Clearly, she's stronger than before and she can float and fly, Kurt is confused but hey, he's seen some crazier and unusual stuff doing this job, so nothing really surprises him now.

Vexor begins to bleed as he is trying to get close enough to enact the plan on his mind. He sees her coming in for another attack and he telegraphs it grabbing her arm and flipping her down on the concrete floor with such force the cracks the floor with her body. Maria is hurt but she knows that she can't let him win. Vexor picks her up by her arm as her body looks limp, he begins to chuckle, his fangs grow from his mouth and he leans in to lay the blow, just then Maria's eyes open and she grabs his jaw. Maria knew this was his last plan and she was ready for him, "That was your plan? Bite me and make me one of you? Or were you going to rip my throat out with your fangs and let me bleed out? You disgust me and I've had enough"

Suddenly Maria's hand that is wrapped around his jaw begins to glow with a mix of red and golden aura and Vexor begins to tremble in fear. Maria begins to syphon back the remaining power from Vexor draining him. Fully drained, she flips out of his grasp with a kick that sends him flying. Maria stands there with the demon's power fully but within her but it's different somehow.

Elizabeth knows this aura well. Explaining out loud, "She's got Scarab Knight blood within her and it was awakened from her when the demon energy was drained; but now she's drained Vexor so she has harnessed both energies within."

Vexor lies there in fear, weakened, and beaten. Maria walks toward him slowly and he feels her powerful presence before she even reaches him. Maria gets to him, grabs him by the throat and us about to finish him, then from nowhere she's hit with a purple fireball. It is Tarok coming from a portal sensing his Master is in danger he shouts, "Take care of those pests trolls and I'll tend to the Master and the Doctor." Out of this portal steps through five werewolves and two Mountain

trolls from the outside battle. Tarok speeds to his Master and speaks, "Master we must regroup, live to fight another dawn."

Vexor looks up at him weakened, "Tarok, how did I lose? I had this victory in the palm of my hands." He looks at the five left standing.  "Yes, let us leave and regroup."

Kurt Danger and his team see what is happening and know they are indeed in trouble. Elizabeth looks at Chuck and says, "This isn't good at all we don't have the strength to fight off one mountain troll let alone two." The mountain trolls roar as they lumber towards the group. Kurt and Baxter see the werewolves and Immediately start firing. The Mountain Trolls swing down they're huge fist onto the floor where Liz once stood. When Liz regains her balance, she begins to conjure energy daggers that have little to no effect on the monstrosities. Chuck begins to fire and sees his bullets bouncing off.

Kurt yells out, "This isn't going to work guys and more of them are coming through. "Out of the purple hole floating in the air comes vampires and werewolves now the group is truly outnumbered.

Just then Maria gets up and moves with lightning speed towards one of the mountain trolls. She hits the beast unexpectedly with such force a chunk of his rocky face flies off and lands on top of a Vampire. That beast drops on its back and Maria then launches herself into the eye of the other troll piercing the beast's eye as it screams out in pain. Chuck and Liz stand there in disbelief. Maria removes her fist from the beast's eye and her arm is covered in orange blood. The beast falls to his knees crying out in pain. Kurt turns to see

Vexor leaving and knows his chance is dwindling. They get up and Tarok opens a portal for them, then he opens one for the Doctor and teleports to grab Doctor Hyde with both of them in tow he summons the power to levitate the Doctor through the portal. Vexor carried by Tarok towards the portal walks weaker than ever before. As they reach Portal opening and begin to step through,

"Vexor!" Kurt screams out his name and Vexor turns to Kurt firing one bullet towards his face with no power left he can't dodge it. Just then Tarok moves him out of the way barely but not before the bullet hits Vexor in his eye. They fall through the portal and it closes.

Kurt screams enraged, "Damnit!"

Baxter grabs his attention, "Kurt they're still coming through. Liz, we need a way out. Now." Just then that golden Scarab construct comes through the portal and flies around Liz and she recognizes it's her cousin's construct. It places itself on her hands and she instantly glows; she throws her hands in the direction of another wall. Just then a portal is opened. She calls out to the rest of them, "Through the portal now!" Maria snaps out of it and lands and goes through the portal first followed by Chuck, Baxter knocks back a werewolf and grabs Kurt and they go through the portal next. Elizabeth then conjures a thousand scarabs to attack the monsters while she runs through the portal closing it behind her.

# Chapter Eleven

# LOOSE ENDS ARE THE HARDEST TO TIE UP

"Kurt, wake up." A soft voice calls out in the pure darkness. The void of darkness stretches out as far as one could see, then lightning flashes and thunder roars around him. Images flash of Maria fighting Vexor, Kurt's ghostly wife, Vexor being shot on the eye, and finally a giant demonic hand outstretched towards Kurt grabbing him dragging him under. Kurt jerks up out of his sleep, looking around realizing he is in a circular room with cobblestone walls all around and symbols of the Scarab Knights. He sees his weapons and clothes in the corner on a table. He also notices the color of the room is a golden hue and the liquid inside of the vessel he was in was also colored golden. The liquid begins to drain out and Kurt stands and gets out of the vessel. Kurt begins to feel around on his body noticing his injuries and wounds are gone. He gets dressed and walks out. Elizabeth is waiting outside the healing chamber. Elizabeth is dressed in a sweater and sweatpants, looking really relaxed from her normal battle gear. She hears the doors open turning around and is immediately pleased. She runs into him hugging him, "Kurt you're alright!" Kurt looks down at her and smiles.

Elizabeth instantly realizes she might've made things awkward; she quickly let's go of her hug clearing her throat. "Glad you're okay. Maria will be ecstatic as well as Baxter. We've all been waiting for you to finally come out of the healing chambers."

Kurt looks at her confused, "How long was I in there Liz?"

Elizabeth looks away for a minute, "We all had to enter healing chambers. 3 days at most for me and Baxter, 4 days for Chuck, and 2 days for Maria. You had more injuries as your body collapsed once we made it out of the castle."

Kurt cuts her off, "How long!"

"Two weeks, you were in there for two weeks Kurt. We didn't know why but my uncle said your soul was weak as well."

Kurt stands there upset, he then looks down at his body whispering, "That's too long."

"What did you say?"

Kurt looks up with anger in his eyes, "That's too long!"

Elizabeth confused, "What are you talking about Kurt?"

Kurt simply says, "Vexor. "

Elizabeth walks away from him in disgust only to turn back pointing him in the chest, "It's over Kurt. We won; can't you see that? Are you that driven by vengeance that you can't see when it's over?"

Kurt grabs her arm as she tries to walk away again, "For you it may be over, but for me it's not over till he's dead. I won't rest till him and his family pays for her death, Samson's death and my mother and father's death."

She grabs his face with both hands and looks him deep in his eyes, "Kurt this will end but not the way you expect, you won't survive this vengeful crusade. I know you know it's true, but if you believe that it will bring you peace, I can't stop you." She kisses his cheek and walks away leaving him in the hallway by himself.

Kurt walks out seconds later towards the cafeteria and he runs into Magnas. Magnas was talking to young scarabs but he stops when he notices Kurt. Telling the young scarabs to go play, he turns to Kurt, "Kurt may I speak with you briefly before you depart?"

Kurt sighs deeply not wanting to talk and walks over to Magnas, "Where's my car?"

Magnas places one hand on Kurt's shoulder, "Kurt before you go, I need to tell you something."

Kurt rolls his eyes, "My car?"

Magnas smiles. "You may not believe it, but you have a greater purpose in this journey. I have seen a vision while you slept. The greater evil needs the girl, his hands stretched out into the void of nothingness towards her. The power she has unleashed has gotten his attention and I fear he will soon show himself and his true form will be revealed. The only way to truly save this world is for you to be there to finish the conflict between the greater evil and the chosen one. Only you can protect her and defeat him, but it will come at a great cost."

Kurt looks at him for a minute in silence. "My car!"

Magnas removes his hand and looks at him pleased, "It lies beneath us in the chambers, our new location is south of Cartersville you can drive out and reach the open road in a few hours. May you find what you seek on this journey so that you can return." He looks at Kurt in his eyes walking towards his chambers.

Kurt makes his way to the lower level where his car resides. Now in the lower level, an ammunition and weapons area, with walls adorned with a variety of weaponry and shelves stocked with even more munitions, spotting his beauty walks over and sees it was repaired. Liz kept her word. He walks up to the driver side and opens the door. He sits in his seat and breathes in deeply happy to be back in his car. He sits there for a minute in a state of peace until Vexor's face flashes across his memory. He then grabs keys out of the sun visor and places the keys in the ignition. The car roars and hums, a pleasant sound to Kurt's spirit.

Baxter knocks on the car door. He walks over to the drivers' side and Kurt looks at him.

For a minute they just stare at each other, "So where we headed?"

Kurt smiles, "Solo mission Wordsworth, Vexor is my problem and now I can finish this once and for all. You are staying with the girls and keeping them safe while I'm gone."

Baxter isn't shocked by what his friend says. He shakes his head, "I'm not going to let you down man. But I have to tell you this won't be easy man you might need some help out there, wherever out there leads you."

Kurt sticks his hand out to shale Baxter's hand, "If I get into a sticky situation, I know how to reach you Bax." Their hands clutch in their handshake, "Promise me you'll keep the girls safe."

Baxter nods, "I promise." Baxter walks away and Kurt shifts the car into drive.

Before he drives off a portal opens up in front of the car and steps out Maria, "Leaving without saying goodbye?" Kurt gets out of the car and Maria runs to him and hugs him tightly. She begins to sob; Kurt holds her chin and wipes away her tears.

"Listen little warrior, I need to finish that bad guy. I need this to make sure it's over. I'm sorry but I thought if I just left you wouldn't hurt so much, and neither would I. But I guess you are too powerful for that little warrior."

Maria smiles, "I like that nickname 'little warrior'. Kurt, do me a favor and kill him. Can you do that and still come back okay?"

Kurt hugs her one more time and gets in the car, "Only if you do me a favor and keep on training and keep Liz and Bax safe till I get back. Deal?"

She walks up to the car window and sticks her hand out for a fist bump. "You got it Kurt." Maria walks into another portal and waves goodbye. Kurt Danger drives off towards his mission.

Deep in a dark dungeon-like area, filled with rats and cobwebs and the stench of the dead, one eye opens up wide. A voice calls out to this person who has awakened from their slumber, "Master you are awake. You're fully healed from your injuries." The blood-filled chamber drains and Vexor rises out of his chamber.

He looks at Hyde and says, "How long?"

Hyde sheepishly replies, "Twwwo weeeks Lord Vexor."

Psychotic laughter fills the cave, "GET OUTTTTTT!" Hyde runs away, Vexor sits there laughing and muttering one name on repeat, "Kurt Danger, Kurt Danger, Kurt Danger."

# Chapter Twelve
# AA MEETING

A black van pulls up to a park area, one man steps out of the car dressed in all black in a black peacoat, black slacks and black shoes with a steel tip. The man walks through the park inconspicuously heading to his meetup destination. The park casted in deep orange and red hues around it as it just turned fall. Thick trees and large rocks and stones are sprinkled throughout. The man walks across a white bridge through an archway into a deeper area of the park. He turns towards benches and finally sees the meeting area. A man sits at a bench all alone in the most vacant part of the park. The man in all black sits down next to the man. The other man dressed in a denim coat with a fur-lined hoodie and he looks much less inconspicuous than his counterpart. The man in the denim slides over a manila envelope to the man in black. The man grabs the folder, opens it up and takes out the paperwork. He begins to thumb through the paperwork, his eyes affixed on every word. He says without turning his head, "This is really damming information, this will lead to the end of the Bureau. But that might be just what is needed to create real change. How'd you get your hands on this information?"

The man in the hoodie replies, "I have my ways. All I need to know is that the information will be used to get rid of the guy at the top. What else you do with it is your business."

The man in black laughs, "What about your friend? You know where he is?"

"Nope."

The man in black smiles, "That's fine. Either way we will have to bring him in. Thanks for this, it will be used effectively. So, what do you want?"

The man in denim gets up, begins walking away, "To be left alone that's all." He calls over his shoulder and before you know it, he's disappeared into the park trees.

At Citadel in her quarters sits Elizabeth with her legs crossed and a book of spells in front of her. Her room is large but still cozy. It has glowing glyphs all over the walls. Her room has this aura to it as it glows in a soft golden tone. She practices her conjuring skills and her hands glow with pulsating energy. She senses another energy enter the room.

"Yes Baxter, can I help you?"

Baxter, taken off guard, begins to laugh.  "I see your powers are improving."

Smiling over at him, "I hear you're leaving too?"

Baxter walks in further, "Yeah figured Magnas would tell you. I have some loose ends to tie up as well. Some questions I need answered. I won't be gone for long a few weeks at best Liz."

She gets up walking over, her hand extended. "Well Mr. Wordsworth I hope you find the answers you are searching for. It's been six months since Kurt left and we have been able to handle things without him so we should be good."

Baxter shakes her hand and smiles, "On that I have no doubt. I'll be back soon though I'll let you know when I'm coming back. Be well Liz." Baxter turns and walks out and heads towards the cafeteria. Baxter runs into Maria eating pancakes, she sees him and gets up to greet him. She runs to hug him, "Hey you're just in time for breakfast."

Baxter kneels down to her and says, "I'll have to take my pancakes to go hun. Gotta go talk with someone important and fix some things. But I couldn't leave without seeing you."

Maria is now upset with him, "First Kurt. Now you. Plus, Kurt isn't even back yet, how will I protect this place all by myself?"

Baxter puts his hand on her shoulder, "You're more than capable of defending this place and besides I won't be long. And hey... if I see Kurt out there, I'll bring his butt back here, okay kiddo?"

Maria smiles at that and says, "You better Bax." With one big hug Baxter heads to the hanger area to leave. Baxter still has some reservations about leaving but knows the answers he needs can only be given by one individual.

*****

In an underground laboratory, Tarok and Dr. Hyde are discussing recent developments. The new laboratory has several giant tubes filled with green and red liquids and various unconscious individuals hooked up to wires and breathing masks. A large monitor in the center of the lab above a console. The doctor is at the console analyzing the data from the bodies within the tubes. Suddenly the door opens and in comes Vexor dressed in an all-black suit and a black and red cape flowing behind him.

He walks up to Tarok and says, "How are the arrangements coming along?"

Tarok replies, "Lord Vexor. Your brother has been notified of your arrival and has accepted your request for an audience with him. Everything is going according to schedule there is just one thing."

Vexor disgusted, "One...one thing? What is it?"

Tarok sheepishly replies, "Kurt Danger has been spotted here in Biertan. There's also been a spike in vampire slayings in several areas."

Vexor slams on the console with his fist, "Danger just won't give up I see. Well then let's prepare a welcome party for him. Tarok you will accompany me to my brother's castle and Dr.

Hyde you will continue work on my projects. Kurt Danger just doesn't know he's a dead man walking."

## TWO WEEKS LATER

A hole in the wall bar in Biertan, Sibiu sits a man in a bar with a large furry coat, a large beard and scraggly hair. He drinks out of a tall beer stein and watches a large group of large men around him drink and speak German. He is listening to their conversations intently; he waits till one of them gets up to go to the restroom. He follows him, when the man sits down on the stall, he barges in and puts his hand on his mouth and a large pistol at his head, he speaks in German, "Listen very closely, if you move I blow your head off then I kill all of your friends out there. You understand?"

He nods. The bearded man continues, "I need you to get me the whereabouts of this woman." He shows him a picture. "You know where she is right?" Again, he nods. "Good very good well then let's have a conversation, my name is Kurt what's yours?"

Kurt Danger kneels down and stares at the individual sitting on the toilet staring at the barrel of his gun, he knows the man's name is Sebastian and he is visibly afraid.

Kurt continues, "So Sebastian where was the last place you've seen the woman in the picture and was there anyone with her?"

Sebastian says to him in German "Sie arbeitet in einem Bordell bei Deva." (She works in a brothel near Deva.)

"Good you're going to take me there. Got it?"

Sebastian shakes his head no, Kurt laughs and says, "Yes you are, Basty ole buddy." Just then Kurt hears the other men in the bar with Sebastian begin to ask what's taking him so long? One of the men begins to make his way towards the bathroom. Kurt looks down at Sebastian, "Hold that thought," slamming his elbow into Sebastian's face knocking him out. Kurt then gets up and goes into another stall and waits for the other guy to come in.

The man's friend comes in and sees the stall open, looks in and sees his friend knocked out. He is confused and begins to shout at him to wake up, just then Kurt comes out and slams the butt of his pistol into the back of his head. Kurt looks at a tattoo on the back of this guy's neck finally noticing these men are Harack bodyguards of Kervon the Tyrant. The one that rules over this city and is Vexor's brother. Kurt now knows he must kill all the men in order to get out of here alive.

He walks out of the bathroom and then men spot him have a stare down and they go to grab their guns, but Kurt pulls his pistol faster shooting both of them in the head. He orders another drink from the visibly scared bartender and walks back into the bathroom to the large men on the floor. One starts to wake up as Kurt shoots him in the back of the head going over to a now awake but slightly groggy Sebastian, Kurt's voice calls out, "Hey let's hit the road Basty." Kurt hits him in his face again knocking him out again. Kurt drags him out of the bathroom, pays the bartender and drinks his beer. Kurt tells the bartender not a word to anyone about this, and then he drags Sebastian out of the bar, picks him up and puts him

into his trunk. Kurt walks around and enters his Black Beauty, turns the engine, looks in his mirror at himself, "I really need to stop drinking."